CALLING DOCTOR B: B For Beware

Georgie Bell

CALLING DOCTOR B

ISBN: 9798315197225

DEDICATION

There is nothing more precious to me than my family. This book is dedicated to them.

CALLING DOCTOR B

CONTENTS

CALLING DOCTOR B

ACKNOWLEDGMENTS

I would like to take this opportunity to thank the whole body of medical staff that worked tirelessly throughout the pandemic. Standing outside on my front doorstep once a week, on Thursday nights at precisely 8pm, clapping for five minutes to show my gratitude, was a small gesture of appreciation; a mere token. I now have a platform to thank you all from the bottom of my heart.

CALLING DOCTOR B

PREFACE

Hi! A few words about me before you read this book. My name is Georgina, Georgie to my friends, and this often gets shortened to G. I'm 42 years old, an outgoing, fun-loving Yorkshire lass, born and bred. I'm a good-humoured, no-nonsense, direct, open and honest sort of person. I regard myself as moderately intelligent and like to keep in shape by fair weather walking in our beautiful Yorkshire countryside. In Winter I hit the gym on average three times a week; aqua aerobics, Zumba, the occasional Spin class. I have a slim/athletic build and am average looking. Definitely comfortable in my own skin. Sounds like an online dating profile!

I don't ask for much. A reliable roof over my head, good job, the means to pay the bills and cover daily expenses. The usual. I have a small family, two parents, three siblings and we all live in close proximity. We get on very well, have our own lives and come together at Christmas, for birthdays, and regular weekend board games and takeaways. Don't get me wrong, things are never perfect; there are squabbles, but never family feuds. Life is sweet.

I don't see my friends as often as I'd like, so make the most of the precious time we do get together. We all have busy lives, daily commitments and like everyone, life's obstacles to manoeuvre. Nothing out of the ordinary.

Having spent a few years living and working abroad, and a failed relationship with a Frenchman behind me (but that's another story!), I returned home to good old Blighty, single and disorientated. Once settled back into my house that I had rented out during my absence, with a new job in a local primary school, I decided I was ready for a serious relationship.

Oh, then there was that little glitch of a pandemic and a global lockdown just to throw a spanner in the works. A worldwide epidemic delayed my plans. During the outbreak of the Covid virus, I became reasonably knowledgeable about gardening and proficient in weeding. In short gardening kept me sane. I emerged from the first lockdown like a butterfly from a chrysalis, with a newfound lust for life and adventure. I was as sociable as ever, arranging nights out with friends, visiting various people for catch ups, dinner and drinks. However, I found the dating pool surrounding my social life somewhat lacking. "Try online dating," said my best friend, Tina. "It's how it's done now. Everyone is meeting via an app. Katie met her current partner online and they are engaged to be married already…" I was reluctant at first, preferring the real world to an unknown virtual reality, but after months of being single, I was fed up with the solitude of lockdown. I decided to give it a go. Multiple first dates lead nowhere, but then perseverance paid off and I was pleasantly surprised to come across a person of interest. Great interest…

1 FIRST CONTACT

I had seen the photograph of a striking gentleman with dark features, a warm smile, six foot tall. I was instantly hooked. He was looking for a serious relationship. Social drinker. Moderate gym goer. Good solid name; Paul. 45 years old. I liked the fact that he was slightly older. After looking at the other photographs on Paul's profile and reading his information, I was convinced that we would be a great match. He was looking for a long-term partner with the aim of establishing a committed relationship. I swiped right and waited with anticipation…a little longer…. anything? Nothing. I felt a little disappointed that our respective pictures did not instantly pop up together with "You've matched!"

I carried on swiping, mostly left, hopeful that I would match with someone who was as equally as compatible as Paul. I must admit, however, with little enthusiasm, after seeing whom I considered my perfect match. I casually sifted through profiles of countless hopefuls (like me) whenever I had a few minutes to spare. I eventually matched with a man who seemed to fit the bill, but to be honest, my heart wasn't in it. He was retired from the army. We exchanged a few texts and arranged to meet at the bistro of my local garden centre. He bought me coffee and later we went Dutch on lunch. It was all very pleasant but there was no real connection. He invited me to his neck of the woods for lunch in Lincoln the following weekend and I agreed, more out of a warped sense of obligation than anything else. I was not feeling over enamored about my second date and continued to check in with the dating app. on a regular basis. Mid-week, there was an unexpected turn of events.

"You've matched!" popped up on the app.

Paul had swiped right. For me. Joy!

The man I was hoping would read my profile and think there was a chance we were as well suited as I did, had matched with me. The man who looked handsome, was well dressed and in theory had a good solid education. A university degree, no less. I was very happy and responded right away.

From the moment I said, "Hi!", the messages flowed, and Paul and I seemed to have an instant connection; We had a lot in common, university background, similar ages, good traditional family values. He was taller than me, so I could easily wear my heels on the many dates we would surely have. Dark hair, dark eyes and a killer smile – Perfect! In his messages, Paul made it abundantly clear that he felt the same.

"I'm so glad we matched," he wrote, "you look so attractive in your pictures."

Right back at ya, I thought, and graciously thanked him for the compliment. "You look nice too in your photos. They look more professional than mine. All my pictures have been taken by friends. I think I was caught off guard in some of them."

"Your profile is very natural. That's what I liked. Your information was open and honest."

"Well, you get what you see with me. I have nothing to hide."

"I also believe we are a good match intellectually and we are both professionals, so we understand the pressures of a stressful workload," added Paul.

The messages continued and over a short period of time became less of an interview type style conversation. Once the boxes on our checklist were ticked, the green flag went up and we gradually eased into a more friendly banter.

We established a comfortable, humorous and warm rapport within no time at all. Paul had me laughing out loud with his funny anecdotes and natural, charismatic style of writing. I had to message the ex-army guy out of courtesy. I apologized for the awkward situation but said that I had met someone else who seemed more compatible. He was thankfully very understanding and wished me luck.

Paul said he was a G.P. and had his own practice. He had worked his way up since obtaining his degree and was now his own boss with a surgery that was conveniently situated opposite the pharmacy in his local village. Medicine was all he had ever known, and Paul opened up about feeling that his life had somehow lacked fun and excitement. After years of studious dedication to a career in medicine, Paul said that he felt he had missed out in life. He had forgone worldly experiences that "normal people" had; going to concerts and festivals, parties, camping. He was well-travelled and had visited many countries, but hadn't experienced the culture on the level he would have liked. He'd mainly gone on cruises where everything was pre-organised and unspontaneous. He said I looked like fun and made it clear that he was physically attracted to my photographs. He thought I had a great outlook on life and believed that I had a colourful wealth of experiences. He described himself as boring. I was pleased that he was not arrogant. There was something humble about the way he spoke about himself. He was evidently successful in his field but took it in his stride. I thought I could inject some fun into his life and show him the wonders of the real world. I was a more spontaneous soul, liked going behind the scenes in any given country. I remember one trip to India we were advised by the tour guide not to eat the street food. Now me being me, I had to try the culinary delicacies. After all, we were at the street food market! Culture wise I loved to stray from the beaten tourist path. Paul loved that about me. He too had been living by the restrictions of the first worldwide lockdown and was keen to find adventure.

I understood that he had spent his life studying hard to become a successful professional. I remembered friends at university who were studying medicine, and they always seemed to be sitting exams. I gave up on asking my medic friend, Claire, if she was coming out at weekends as she was constantly studying for the next set of examinations. I enjoyed quite a different university life. I was out to make the most of the social side of things. Don't get me wrong, I made sure that I completed all my assignments and met deadlines as I was determined to come out with a degree. However, I never missed out on a social occasion. Student nights in the various clubs were always great fun and I loved all the house parties.

Paul had been married previously. His marriage had lasted almost twenty years, and in his messages, he made it clear that he was put into a position where he absolutely had to leave because life became intolerable. In short, his ex-wife was mad and at times quite violent. Paul explained to me that after dating for a while their respective families started putting on pressure for them to get engaged and later married. He said that it had basically been an arranged marriage that he had never wanted to happen. The families expected it and as his parents were ailing, Paul wanted to appease them. Within months his wife became pregnant, and Paul realised that there was no turning back. I felt instantly sorry for him, on hearing this, enduring such a difficult situation "for the children's sake." Paul had two children; a son and a daughter, who had both left university with top class degrees. His daughter Anna had recently qualified as a lawyer and his son, Kiko, was an established dentist. They were both independent and led very busy lives.

This sounds too good to be true, I thought at the time. A doctor, a lawyer and a dentist – Wow! Now that's an impressive family. I recall meeting up with a close friend, Tina, and filling her in on my news. We met up for a coffee and had a stroll around the local park where she lived. We had only communicated via telephone calls during lockdown, so we always had lots to talk about when we did meet up face to face.

"I've met someone." I said, almost whispering.

"What? How? Who is he?" Tina squealed with excitement.

There had been a distinct absence of gossip during the last year. The highlight of our week had been the deathrate updates on the News. I stopped watching it after a while, it was all so depressing. I turned my focus towards tending my garden.

"We've met online. His name is Paul. He's a doctor but we haven't met yet."

I expressed my skepticism about the match as it all seemed, well, just too good to be true. This was the first time that I had felt excited about matching online. I hoped that it wasn't a fake profile. Tina reminded me that I was new to the dating scene and was naturally cautious about meeting people online. She advised that I should go with the flow and avoid jumping to any conclusions before spending some time with Paul. "Enjoy it," she said, "Just go with it." He sounds nice, from what you have said, you sound well-suited.

He's probably had a rough time of it during his marriage, so you will be his breath of fresh air. You've been waiting for someone intelligent with a good job. Paul could be your person."

Paul could be my person. I hoped so.

"OK. I'll enjoy it. It might not last forever, or even get off the ground, but yes, I'll dive in and give it a go." Paul had a way of putting me at ease and instilling confidence. He made the altogether daunting experience of online dating, which was totally alien to me, really quite pleasant. He seemed lovely. I would stop second guessing and cease creating problems where they did not exist. I was determined to make a go of this. I would indeed go with the flow, play it cool, and have zero expectations.

Paul suggested that we face time, so a date was set for a video call, which was the natural next step for me. I was still rather daunted at the prospect of having any kind of rapport with a complete stranger. Although we had been messaging for a few weeks, how well did I know this man?

I had been single for two years before signing up to the online dating site. I did not particularly enjoy the repetitive, arduous selection process. Endless matches, messages, inevitably ending in being ghosted. I preferred to meet people in person. I was quite outgoing and loved socialising. That's exactly why I agreed to meet Lincoln man (I've forgotten his name). I hated texting, even people that I knew. I would always call friends after three or four texts. It just felt easier and less impersonal. I had heard the usual horror stories about online dating experiences. People could be absolutely anyone they wanted to be. They could create a false persona, an alter ego. I hoped that Paul would look and sound at least similar to how I had imagined him. I had already built up an image in my head of what he would look like and how he would speak. I hoped that the video call would not disappoint.

2 VIDEO CALL

I took some time deciding what to wear for the call. I was used to making myself look presentable from the waist up. We all were. Most of us were well-groomed, dressed in nice clothes as far as our upper bodies were concerned, with the added quirky tradition of pyjama bottoms. This was what it meant to be camera ready in 2020. I made sure that my hair and make-up were immaculate, eager to make a good first impression. I positioned my device on top of the mantelpiece and tried various positions with the chair. I would look upwards towards the screen for the best camera angle and flattering appearance, no double chin that way. I had nervous butterflies and kept checking the time. I hoped that Paul met my expectations and was praying that his online pictures weren't twenty years out of date. I was also crossing my fingers that Paul would like *me* and that I would live up to *his* expectations of the "attractive profile pictures" that he said had lured him in.

Sure enough, Paul was as handsome on screen as his photos, a true reflection of his profile pictures, if not better. He was well-spoken, obviously well-educated, confident and very funny. He got up from his cream leather sofa at one point and started walking around the house downstairs. From his living room where he had been sitting, he moved to the open-plan kitchen-diner and then into the hallway. He proceeded into another living room. It was all very spacious and well, big. He was wearing trousers, not pyjama bottoms, I noticed. I had luckily put on a pair of black jeans, just in case. I didn't want to get caught out by my amateur filming. Paul then continued to provide an unprompted tour of his house, which I believed to be a strange thing to do for someone he had never met, but we were all acting strangely after having experienced a futuristic kind of 1984 lifestyle where real-life social interaction had not been permitted for a few months.

Paul evidently felt confident enough to trust me to look around each room in turn. I suppose I was like a guest, who in the real world, would have been invited in. I remember thinking at the time, I am looking to potentially date you, not buy a house from you. It was odd and unexpected. Nevertheless, I was open-minded and non-judgmental. He was proud of where he lived, and rightly so as it was a lovely, modern house. Paul moved past more matching cream leather lounge suite furniture, and he guided me round the spacious living room that looked out onto the back garden. I chose my own house based on the fact that the living room was not directly at the front of the house, on show to the world. As Paul walked back into his kitchen, which also seemed very large, I noticed that it was whiter than white. His pearly kitchen units were sparkling. He kept a clean and tidy house and had good taste. He was classy. He then walked into an additional lounge area towards the front of the house, still no sign of any doors. The place looked enormous. There was a huge wall-mounted television set and yet another massive cream leather sofa. Everything looked shiny and new, with minimalist décor in neutral colours and a degree of formality. It looked like a show house; it had a certain clinical appearance. Everything in its place, pristine and perfect. This was in complete contrast to my colourful and casual bohemian style. I later learnt that he had employed an interior designer to kit out the place. I, on the other hand, just flashed at him a few fleeting images of my living room, where I happened to be making the call, thinking I should have perhaps tidied up in advance and made the room look more presentable. My pad looked, well, homely and lived in. I was, after all, expecting a facetime date, not a house exchange encounter. Paul was keen to make a good first impression. It was his way of showing me what he had to offer, displaying his assets. I could tell that he was trying hard to impress me, more so as we were not meeting in person. It was clear to me that he was interested. Now, I am not the easiest of people to impress, if I am honest, but he did leave me with a very positive overall picture of his lifestyle and personality. He complimented me, saying that I was very pretty on screen and that my photographs on the app. did not do me justice. He was keen to meet up in person and was forthright in fixing up a proper lunch date in the real world. As he lived in Nottingham and I was on the other side of Sheffield, in Holmfirth. We weren't too far from each other. I had studied in Nottingham, so could relate to places he talked about. I could picture where his house and surgery were, and this satisfied me that he was who he claimed to be. All the locations that he spoke of checked out in my mind. There was a degree of familiarity, and I liked that.

Our verbal conversation flowed even more easily than our text messages. We both said that it was like chatting with an old friend. We had lost a good few months in lockdown and were champing at the bit to get out and about again. Paul concluded that I was a social butterfly after hearing about some of my escapades pre-Covid. We exchanged lockdown tales of woe, and both agreed that we were ready for adventure.

The following Saturday we would meet in person at the shopping centre between our respective towns. He would make the longer journey from his side, and I would travel the 20 minutes from where I lived. I would feel **safe** as there would be plenty of people around and if it was raining, we would stay warm and dry within the comfort of the enormous indoor venue.

Wonderful. I was really looking forward to our first date, I was buzzing like a bee. How exciting!

3 THE REAL WORLD

I arrived at the shopping centre in good time, so as not to be late and disappoint. I already really liked Paul. I wanted to make the best impression possible, but didn't want to get to the rendez-vous point too early, so I wandered around, browsing, window shopping, until I felt it was time to make my way to the meeting place, in front of the indoor fountain. I had always taken the fountain for granted, but it gave me great pleasure to see it again. It felt good to be back. Back out and about. There was a degree of novelty value being in the shopping centre after spending so much time adhering to the rules of essential shopping only. The restrictions allowed very little in the way of freedom. I enjoyed roaming around the various familiar shops, but didn't dare touch anything. There was a "no try on" policy in most shops. The stores where you could try on clothes had to quarantine them immediately afterwards if you decided not to buy. It was easier and less hassle for everyone to just browse. The staff were all still wearing face masks. Customers were not required to, but some people felt safer in doing so. It all felt very strange. Familiar but weird. I had a spare mask in my coat pocket, but I wasn't going to wear it for my first real date with Paul.

I was consciously going to try and play it cool, but I knew it was not in my nature to be mysterious and aloof. I messaged that I had arrived, and Paul replied immediately that he was also already in the shopping centre. He had parked in the furthest possible car park, not knowing the centre like I did, and was walking towards the fountain, in my direction. I eagerly awaited his arrival. About a minute later my phone rang. It was Paul. He said he was almost there and could see me. As I turned around, I saw a small male figure in the distance, wearing an overcoat and a beanie, phone to his ear. Is that him, I wondered? He looks short… perhaps he looks short because he's far away, maybe it's not him. As the man approached, he waved and smiled while we were still connected on the phone. Right, this is it, that's definitely him. We both hung up and said Hi. Face to face. Person to person.

"Erm…Paul…?" I hesitated.

"Yes. Hi, how are you?"

I was a little taken aback. This guy was definitely not much taller than me, let's cut the pleasantries. "I thought you were six foot tall!" I exclaimed. I could not hide my surprise. It was the first thing that jumped out of my mouth.

"I am!" he replied confidently. He was self-assured and seemed convinced that he was actually six foot.   Was he delusional?   Was this his sense of humour?

I was somewhat puzzled. "You can't possibly be six foot because you are no taller than me and I am five foot six," I said, squaring up to him and looking him directly in the eye.

He laughed and said, "Well I was six foot the last time I got measured …perhaps age has shrunk me, you hear of people shrinking as they get older." He smiled. Did I mention he had a lovely smile? To say that he was stretching the truth is an understatement. He probably wished he were taller. I'd heard of men exaggerating their height online in order to get matches, as many women, me included, were looking for men taller than themselves. He seemed so nice. His eyes were gorgeous. Was I really that bothered about his height? I suppose I felt a little sorry for him. He wanted me to believe that he was taller than his real height.

He gently nudged my arm. "Let's go and get a coffee." I was happy that he took the initiative and gladly agreed with a big smile. Keep calm, stay cool, I told myself. Don't appear too keen. We had lots to say to each other and there appeared to be a mutual interest in one another, asking more details about personal interests, hobbies, family and work. I was interested in Paul's work as my father had worked in the medical profession, before taking retirement. I was familiar with Paul's potential work commitments. He said he did not have a lot of time to date, and he found it difficult to meet people due to his busy schedule. Covid had meant that he had been even busier. I also had a demanding workload and was dictated to by fixed hours and school routines, so we both understood this aspect of our professions. Paul told me that he was free at certain points in the week as well as weekends and it matched well with my own availability. So far so good, I thought. It was all going well.

On finishing our coffee, Paul asked if I wanted to go for lunch. I accepted politely and we walked around the various food outlets and decided to go with an Italian option. We ordered a pizza to share and continued our animated conversation. Things were going well.

"How much do you think my watch is worth?" Paul asked, out of the blue.

"I have no idea," I replied. "I don't really have much idea regarding the value of wrist watches."

"Go on, have a guess." He invited.

"I really have no clue."

"Just as a game, what would you say?"

I played along as he seemed insistent, "two thousand pounds." I thought a doctor with an expensive watch was acceptable. 2K was a reasonable guess.

"Try again".

Should I go higher or lower? Probably higher…., "Four thousand pounds." That should do it.

"No, guess again."

Jesus! It's some expensive watch…. maybe a Rolex or something…. Just be silly and guess a higher amount, play along. Go for it, G! Paul seemed to enjoy keeping me guessing. "Twenty thousand pounds." Ridiculous, I thought.

"Sixty."

"Sixty pounds," I laughed. "I am not into expensive watches either". Silly me, I should have known. He was wearing a pair of black jeans and a simple navy T-shirt, by no means ostentatious.

"Sixty thousand."

Silence.

"SIXTY THOUSAND POUNDS?" My eyes widened and mouth opened. Not a good look. Sort yourself out, G. Classy and demure mind set re-set.

"I'm sorry, sixty thousand pounds?" I repeated, less dramatically.

"Yes, I like my watches. This is one of my favourites."

"Well, it's a lovely watch and if that's what you choose to spend your money on, that's up to you. You work hard. It's your money after all. Fair enough." I was rather surprised that someone would spend so much money on a wristwatch but made no judgement call. "Just one of many expensive watches," I logged. Men, cars and watches! It didn't really matter to me. He could have been wearing a candy watch from the sweet shop for all I cared. When I looked into Paul's deep dark eyes as he spoke, he had me hooked.

The date continued into the afternoon and after our final coffee Paul took the initiative without hesitation. "Let's visit Matlock for our next date", he said confidently, "we can have a wander around, go for a drink, maybe a bite to eat." I liked that he took charge, he was decisive and charismatic.

"Lovely idea. Yes, let's meet up in Matlock and have a day out." I replied with glee.

Paul leaned in towards me and I had a moment of uncertainty. That moment when you wonder if it's going to be a hug…or a kiss…He came in closer and put his arms around me. As he gave me a hug, our cheeks brushed together, and I snuggled into his chest. "I can tell by that hug that you want to see me again." He said smugly. He was right, I definitely did. He was gorgeous. But I nipped myself for not playing it cool as we said goodbye. I wanted to say something smart and witty in response, but nothing came to mind.

As we left each other's company I felt like I was floating on air. I had met "my person," I was sure of it. Perhaps a shorter version than anticipated, but you know the saying about height not being an issue when you're lying down. Although I did find it odd that we had had the guess how much my watch is worth conversation. My subconscious parked that for later. I put it down to Paul wanting to impress, like when he'd given me the virtual tour of his lovely house. I assumed that it was Paul displaying his peacock plumage.

I wandered around the shopping centre for a while, not having been out and about much recently due to the dreaded C word. I was in no rush to get home. I enjoyed the gentle buzz of the somewhat diminished crowd compared to pre-C. About two hours later, I decided to head home. When I got in, I checked my phone. There would be no messages from Paul, I knew it was way too soon to expect any kind of communication already. We'd only just parted ways.

7 missed calls. All from Paul!

I was surprised and rang straight back. "Is everything OK? I've got several missed calls from you."

"I was worried, sweetheart. I was checking to see if you had arrived home safely. I know you haven't driven for a while."

"I'm fine. I've been driving to work for key worker children duty, so I'm not out of the habit. That's so lovely of you making sure I'm OK." Paul made me feel safe, cared for and protected. He was so lovely.

"Why didn't you answer your phone?" He asked curiously.

"I'm not attached to my phone like some people are. Plus, I didn't hear it in the shopping centre."

"You didn't go straight home?" He seemed surprised.

"No. I wanted to make the most of my get out of jail free pass. You never know how long this new freedom is going to last. I haven't been out for ages, let alone shopping."

"Did you buy anything nice?"

"No, I just wandered round, enjoying being, well just out of the house, a change of scenery, you know? For future reference, I don't take my mobile everywhere I go, so don't be perturbed if I don't answer immediately. In fact, I often refer to my mobile as my 'static'. I waited for the laughing response to my poor joke. OK, it was awful.

"Well, as long as you're OK, sweetheart. I'll message you in the week to confirm the arrangements for our date on Saturday. I finish early, so we can meet early in the afternoon if you like and have dinner later." There was a certain business-like manner to the arrangements, but that was often Paul's style. He ran his own medical practice and had several staff working for him. He needed to be logical and methodical.

"That will be lovely. I'm already looking forward to it."

"Me too. Bye, sweetheart."

4 "PAUL"

Date two took us to the lovely town of Matlock. I was very late as the journey took longer than I had anticipated. I stopped and pulled up twice to ring Paul to let him know that I would be late. He was really laid back and relaxed about it. "Take your time, sweetheart, no rush. I'll have a coffee while I'm waiting."

When I eventually arrived, I didn't have any change for the parking metre but thought, who's checking? Hardly anyone is here. Everywhere is short staffed at the moment, I'll risk it. A lot of the population either had Covid, were isolating with symptoms, or were working from home. When Paul saw me in the car park, he came up to me and the first thing he asked was, "Have you paid and displayed?"

"No, I've been cashless for the last year and don't have a bean on me and the machine only takes coins."

"I've got some change, I'll sort it." He went directly to the parking meter and paid for my ticket.

"You don't want to get caught out," he warned, "I got a ticket here two weeks ago."

"Oh, you were here recently?"

"Yes, I came a couple of weeks ago on a date, but it didn't go anywhere. We weren't suited. But I risked not paying the parking and got a ticket."

Bad Karma, I thought to myself. But then I almost made the same mistake. Mmmm I was not Paul's only potential partner. I was not as unique and special as I had imagined. Paul was dating other people. But then I had met up with someone only a couple of weeks before meeting Paul, so I guess we were even.

I felt a thin wall go up on hearing that Paul had been dating so recently, and moreover, during the time that he had been messaging me. But it was early days and that's how dating worked nowadays, so I tried to let it go. My spider sense was definitely tingling, however. I didn't like the thought of being one of many. I wanted to be someone's one and only. That went on the back burner, to smolder away.

As Paul had paid for coffee and then insisted on lunch being his shout at the shopping centre, I thought I would surprise him. He was looking for fun and adventure, so I had booked a cable car ride for us. We had a stroll around the park, then at around 2pm I suggested going for a coffee in the cute little tearoom in the park. Time flew by as we chatted and caught up about our week. Nothing out of the ordinary. Before I knew it, I was urging Paul to gulp down his second cup of coffee and finish his cake. I had booked the cable car for 3pm, so we needed to be making our way to the entrance. He still had no idea what I had planned. "What's the rush? Where are we going? This is intriguing."

When we arrived, we were asked by the lady at the entrance if we had pre-booked our tickets as they had sold out the few places that were available. Paul looked at me and shrugged his shoulders, "Oh, we didn't know…What a shame, sweetheart." He went to respond to the lady, "No…. we…"

"Yes," I cut in and I held out the two "golden" tickets I had printed off earlier that day. I had such a massive grin on my face. I was so pleased with myself. Smug even. I was on the ball.

"When did you book those?" Paul asked in amazement.

"Last week. I've been plotting."

"That's very clever of you, G. Well done!" He was impressed.

Paul insisted on giving me the money for the tickets, but I said that as he had bought lunch on our first date, it was only fair that I treated him in return.

"OK, just this once, but next time you book something, let me know and I'll give you the money."

We got off the cable car and I suggested that we go to visit the caves. "Definitely, I'll follow you. I'm having such a lovely day," said Paul. "You *are* fun!" During the course of the day my thin wall gradually began to lower.

"I can't believe you've never done the caves or the cable car. What have you done previously when you've been to Matlock?"

"I tend to just sit in the pub, nothing as exciting as this."

"Well, I've not been out for months and I'm not a sit in the pub all day kind of person. I used to plan and organise school trips before we weren't allowed to travel, and restrictions spoilt our fun. I used to love doing that."

"Well, you can do all the organising and planning for our holidays, then."

"Holidays?" I beamed with delight.

"Absolutely. Now we can travel and get out and about, we'll go on lots of adventures. As the restrictions lift we can see the world together."

"That's music to my ears, Paul. I love to travel and visit new places. My ex was very much a homebody and didn't like travelling much, well, at all. He wouldn't even come to England to visit my family." We had talked about our respective ex partners; Paul's mad ex-wife and my French cop. I had told Paul how I had moved to France with all the optimism in the world of an exciting life in Paris, but the reality had been far from glamorous. My relationship with Gerard had come to an inevitable bitter end, I explained.

"Well, there's no stopping *us* now, I am semi-retired and have all the time in the world for holidays. We can go anywhere you like."

"Fantastic!" I enthused. "The only thing is, *I* am *not* semi-retired, in fact I'm quite a long way off retirement, so I'm tied to school holidays….and flights and accommodation tend to be more expensive at that time."

"Don't worry, it *will* be more expensive, but I'm not strapped for cash. I can pay for our holidays."

"Oh, no, I didn't mean that. I can pay my own way, I just meant that we will be tied to fixed times of the year and the travel agents don't half take advantage."

"Well, I do work the odd day here and there at the surgery, so I still have a duty to my patients….so I could only ever do a week or so at any given time anyway."

"It all sounds like everything will fall into place nicely, then." We both smiled and Paul put his arm around me and kissed my cheek gently. I blushed as I gently chuckled to myself with contentment.

By this time, we were both feeling hungry. "Let me call a cab," said Paul in an assertive manner. "A taxi? Let's walk, it's not far." I suggested dropping down into the town itself in search of somewhere to eat. "That's refreshing," said Paul. "My ex always demanded that we get a taxi everywhere."

"Did you have the children with you at that time?" I asked.

"No, my ex, not my ex-wife. She was very lazy."

"I didn't know you'd had a relationship after your divorce."

"Well, my relationship with Mel was ill-fated from the start. She was absolutely stark raving bonkers. What a waste of ten years that was." I noticed that Paul's mood started to sink and the atmosphere in our bubble of happiness suddenly felt a little heavy.

"Well, let's enjoy *our* day out." I endeavoured to lighten and brighten up the ambience. "We can have the "ex conversation" at a later date." My brain began to process the information and although I'm no mathematician, the numbers did not make sense. Paul was 45, married for twenty years, had a relationship for ten years in addition to that…Things did not add up.

"Agreed! Enough of them, let's focus on us."

 We ambled round the pretty town and Paul took my hand. Despite the mention of mad Mel, it felt very romantic. We chose a restaurant to have dinner, and the staff there were more than welcoming as we were their only customers. Once the food had been ordered, Paul took a deep breath in and sighed. He leant towards me, and from nowhere, whispered "I'm not Paul."

"What?" I wasn't sure that I'd heard him correctly.

Slightly louder, Paul announced that "Paul" was in fact not his real name. As you can imagine, I was taken aback, particularly as we had been messaging for quite a while by now, speaking on the phone and had already had our first date.

"My name is Ravi, but you can call me "Rav". All my patients call me Doctor B."

"Oh," I exclaimed, "I thought you were called Paul."

"Yes, Paul is my online name just in case any of my patients recognise me."

It seemed acceptable that he should adopt a false name as he was a professional working in the public eye. I understood.

"So, what does the B stand for?" I asked.

"Bhavantananda." He replied. "But no one can ever pronounce that, so I'm known as Doctor B."

"Gosh, that's a mouth full. I can see why your patients call you Doctor B. It's quite catchy."

I burst into song; "Won't you help me Doctor B, Doc, Doc, Doc Doc, Doctor B." I laughed and asked if he knew the song. He hesitated and said not. I explained that it was actually Doctor Beat, but they sounded similar.

"You're funny," he laughed.

"My surname is easy to remember. It's Bell."

"Georgie Bell! That has a good ring to it! Get it?" He laughed loudly, believing he had cracked the best joke in the world.

"Mmmm," I rolled my eyes, "I haven't heard that one before."

Paul, correction, Ravi continued, "Georgie, that name rings a bell!" and he laughed even louder, as though he had invented the very saying himself.

Did he really think he had made an original discovery? Surely not. Anyway, I left it. I had other things on my mind. I was puzzled.

"Are you really 45?" I asked curiously.

He laughed and replied, "Of course, I know I look young for my age but that's the aesthetics." I wasn't sure what age to put on my profile as I thought people wouldn't believe me." *I didn't believe him. Who gets married at fifteen years old!*

"Aesthetics?" I queried. "Have you had work done on your face?"

"Yes, it's my job. I need to look the part, or my clients wouldn't have confidence in me."

"Clients?" I was confused.

"Yes, my clients that come to the beauty clinic."

"Oh, I thought you were a doctor, as in a G.P?"

"Yes, I am. Don't worry. That's true. I do aesthetics on the side in addition to my role as a G.P. When we are allowed to do cosmetics again, that will eat up my Wednesday afternoons and Saturdays as things get back to normal."

"I guess you are more qualified than most to be doing that kind of work. My hairdresser once asked me after my cut and blow-dry if I would like Botox in the basement of her salon, but I wasn't exactly instilled with confidence."

"Did you have anything done?"

"No, I wouldn't dare. It's not my thing. I believe in the natural look; age gracefully and all that. I don't actually think I need anything doing, so I was a little taken aback when she asked."

"Oh, don't worry, I'll sort you out. You're going out with an aesthetician now." Paul, I mean Ravi winked reassuringly.

"No, don't feel obliged. I'm fine as I am," I interjected before he said any more. "I'm happy with myself, comfortable in my own skin." I smiled. The cosmetics conversation had completely washed away my mathematical calculations.

He said no more about the matter, and I thought to myself; Doctor B…. B for Botox. There is more to this guy than meets the eye. I secretly nicknamed him Doctor Botox that night in the restaurant.

We continued to chat into the night and Paul, I mean Ravi, suggested that we have a weekend away as our next step forward. This was a bit fast paced for me, so I asked if it was OK with him if we booked two separate rooms. He was, after all, still a relative stranger, as far as I was concerned. Something felt uneasy. Ravi was not Paul. I was convinced that he couldn't possibly be 45. Paul, sorry Ravi, (it took some time to get used to) agreed and instantly put me at ease once again. He was so kind and understanding and extremely generous. I loved his calm, gentle manner. He said that I should choose somewhere, pay with my card and he would give me the cash. He said that he had every faith in me being a great events organiser based on what I had told him about my travel experiences. He was right, I loved to research places and book activities. I was good at putting together a schedule and incorporating a varied mix of things to do, visit and see. I was queen of the itinerary.

We agreed on a trip to the Lake District. Not too far away and perfect for a weekend getaway.

Friday afternoon arrived and the plan was for Ravi to meet me at my house and then he would drive us up to the Lakes. He was bang on time. No sooner had he pulled onto the drive in his gleaming white BMW, than my suitcase was in the boot. We set off straight away, chatting and giggling together. Excited about the weekend.

We arrived at the glorious location and enjoyed the scenery surrounding the BnB as we walked down the path to reception. We were so happy. It was idyllic. As we checked in, the receptionist asked uncertainly, "Two rooms?" Ravi hesitated, "Erm, I think it's just the one room."

"Well… no," I interrupted awkwardly, we had after all agreed on two separate rooms. It was an uncomfortable silence. I think everyone in the reception area heard the silence. Then the receptionist tried rather clumsily to help. She suggested that we have a think about it. Ravi took one look at me, saw how ill at ease I was and confirmed, "Two rooms. We'll take two rooms. That is what we agreed."

He lowered his voice as he turned to me, "I thought you were joking."

"Sorry." I shrugged, but a deal is a deal, n'est-ce pas?

Once we had got over the awkwardness of the room situation, we did in fact have an absolutely amazing weekend. Ravi invested in a brand-new pair of walking boots. I believe that's the only time he ever wore them. We went on glorious hikes. The weather was perfect; mild and dry. We had romantic candlelit dinners and at the end of the night, we struggled to leave each other and go to our respective rooms. But we did.

Ravi dropped me off at home on his way back down to Nottingham and before we said our goodbyes, he asked, "Next time one room?"

I agreed and nodded, "One room."

It was down to me to organise our next weekend away. This time we were going a little further afield, to Scotland. One room…this was it! I had been single, very single, for two years and so the next step to our relationship was important to me. Time to pack the lingerie!

5 LOCKDOWN

We were both looking forward to our next weekend away. I had found a charming BnB, booked one room, as agreed, with a garden view, and I had even started to plan my outfits. But our weekend in Scotland was not meant to be as our Prime Minister, Mr. Boris Johnson, had other plans. A few days before our trip, a second lockdown was announced.

I was so disheartened. I'd already spent one lockdown alone, in isolation, only speaking with people as they passed the house to walk their dogs. Tina came by on the day of my birthday on her way to the supermarket. She threw a card over the fence, and we chatted from a distance through the iron bars of the railings that surrounded my back garden. I was one of the lucky ones. I had a beautiful garden. I think I would have lost my sanity had I not had this treasured outdoor space. My prison was more than adequate than most.

"You have no choice, sweetheart," Ravi said on the phone. "You'll have to come and stay here at the house. You'll have to move in."

He was right. If this relationship was going to work, I had to basically move in. I lived alone, so I had no ties. I worked in Nottinghamshire, so it made sense for me to live at Ravi's. That way I wouldn't have to worry about crossing county lines going to and from work or feel anxious about being stopped by the Covid police if I wanted to see Ravi. There had been stories on the news of people being fined for not adhering to the rules. We had all stayed at home to protect the NHS and been good citizens. Well, most of us had, but not all of us, we learnt when we came through it all at the other end. I was determined to do the right thing. If Ravi and I were going to make it, we had to take the next step. We were going to share a room together in Scotland, we would just have to accelerate time.

Relationships were tested to the max at that time. People had to make decisions about where to be locked down. Newly formed couples were forced into making premature decisions on whether or not to move in together. The population had to make decisions fast. I wasn't going to let this opportunity slip through my fingers. We chose to take the plunge. I moved into Ravi's.

We were both kept busy during the week. Ravi continued to go into the surgery, and I taught online. Cosmetics were deemed unnecessary, so Ravi had Wednesday afternoons and Saturdays free. We spent entire weekends of quality time together. It was perfect. We soon found a routine of weekend walks in the park and went into town on foot for extra exercise for the food shopping.

One night when we were sharing a bottle of red wine, I caught Rav off guard. "So how old are you really?" I had bided my time but had not forgotten the unsolved mathematical problem.

"Forty-five", he slurred.

"I know you're not. There's no way you got married at fifteen. How old were you when you got married?"

"Twenty." He laughed into his glass.

"That's so young! So that makes you at least...fifty! Oh my God, you're in your fifties!"

"I'm fifty." Ravi said, nodding his head.

Age doesn't bother me, but I was surprised that Ravi had lied so blatantly and now, for so long.

"Why did you lie to me? You know I wouldn't be bothered. I much prefer the truth to dishonesty. We need to be honest with each other and build trust if our relationship is going to last."

"I know you're right," agreed Ravi. "I'd already given you a false name, so I wanted to leave it a while before I told you my real age. Time went by and then it seemed unimportant, and I didn't regard it as an issue."

"And it's not an issue. It's just not the best way to start a relationship. Is there anything else I should know? Be honest with me."

"No, I promise, sweetheart. That's it."

"Let's forget about it then, PAUL!" I joked. I couldn't resist having a little dig.

"Shall we take this wine up to bed? We can watch a movie afterwards."

"After the wine?" I giggled, pulling his leg.

"I...er..." he stammered.

"I know, silly. I'm messing with you." And I swished past him, swinging my hips, saying, "Ooh la la" in my best French accent, on my way upstairs.

True to nature, during the next few weeks, that turned into months, I would organise intimate quiz games, set up comedy challenges, plan indoor/outdoor treasure hunts, depending on the weather. There were also numerous kitchen disco parties, cocktail evenings and more. We would watch videos on how to make different recipes and then have a cook-off. We played lawn volleyball, went on mystery tour walks, and even attempted to take up jogging. Ravi was always astounded at how creative I was. He loved it all. It served as a respite from the awful circumstances at work. Ravi was having most of his appointments online and said that people were struggling. Some, particularly the elderly, just wanted a chat as they were really lonely.

We would talk about places we wanted to visit and things we had on our bucket list. Ravi wanted to learn to fly a helicopter, maybe a plane. I wanted to go to México for Día de los Muertos. Ravi wanted to return to his life of cruises. I was up for giving a cruise a chance. We both wanted to visit the Amalfi Coast; one of the few places that neither of us had visited.

I started a book of bucket list plans, printed off pictures and stuck them onto the relevant pages, kind of like an old-fashioned scrapbook. I presented it to Ravi one evening when he came home looking dismayed.

"This is so lovely, Georgie. We have so much to look forward to, sweetheart." He looked slightly happier as he turned each page.

On another occasion Ravi came home and said he had a surprise for me. He looked at the ceiling lighting in the living room and said, "Come with me." He led me into the kitchen.

"This is saucy," I giggled. "Are we covering each other in chocolate spread or honey?"

"Neither. Sit down." He grabbed a kitchen chair and positioned it directly under the light, examining my face as he turned to look at the light again.

"Intriguing. What do you have in mind?"

"Stay there." And he disappeared out the front door and I heard the car door slam. He appeared seconds later with a small box.

"I'm going to do your face." He said with a big smile.

"What? What do you mean, do my face?"

"I've brought some Botox from the surgery so we can do your face."

"But I don't want my face doing. There's nothing wrong with my face. Don't you like me as I am?" I could feel myself getting upset and started to feel a little panicked. Didn't Ravi like me the way I was? He had said that he found me attractive. He had chosen to date me. Why had he continued to e me if he wasn't happy with the way I looked?

"I don't want to change how I look. I like who I am." For the first time in our relationship, I started to cry.

Ravi said he just wanted to enhance what I already had. He said that any other woman would beg him to work his magic on their face. I told him by all means to beautify his clients with Botox, but he was not coming anywhere near my face with a needle.

"Ah, well, if that's what you want. I have women pleading with me to do cosmetics during lockdown. I've had to turn them all down because we aren't allowed to practice aesthetics. You don't know how lucky you are."

I was not convinced. I felt sad and dejected, sitting in the chair, under the harsh light of the stark white kitchen.

"You don't realise what you are refusing. I'll put it in the fridge in the garage if you change your mind."

"I won't," I shouted after him as he left with the box. Doctor B's bloody

Botox box. He can keep his bloody box of tricks. I'm no human pin cushion.

The matter was soon forgotten about, and we re-established our rapport and returned to our fun times together. It was, however, another issue that I had stored in the recesses of my mind. I wasn't going to be one of Doctor Botox's patients. I was his girlfriend, not his client.

We had a daffodil planting bonding session, another one of my surprise activities. I did most of the weeding and planting, and Ravi poured the wine. We were back on track.

Christmas arrived and Ravi's children were keen for him to spend Christmas with them. I wanted to see my family, so according to the Rule of Six, we spent a couple of days apart. I went to mum and dad's in Holmfirth and Ravi stayed in Nottingham and spent Christmas at Anna's where Kiko joined them. Ravi rang me on Christmas day morning to wish a very merry Christmas to me and my family. When I asked him how his children were and how his day was going, he gave a massive sigh. "Not great. The kids' mother turned up on the doorstep last night, demanding to spend Christmas with them. They hadn't seen her for a while and as it was unannounced, they weren't impressed. She said she was their mother and demanded to be part of their Christmas bubble."

"Oh, I didn't realise you'd be spending Christmas day with your ex-wife." You can imagine my dismay.

"Well, it's never going to happen again because the children have already had enough of her. All she does is bicker and pull me down. It's no fun for Kiko and Anna. She's already ruined their Christmas…and mine"

"That's awful. You'll just have to bite the bullet and get on with it. Be there for your children, it's only a couple of days."

"Yes, you're right, of course. It'll all soon be over. I'm not spending Christmas like this next year. 2021 is going to be different."

"Well, that's a long way off. Try and have a good Christmas. Don't take the bait. I'll see you soon." I didn't relish the thought of Ravi and his ex-wife in the same house for Christmas, but it definitely did not sound like a great place to be.

As I hung up, I couldn't help but thank my lucky stars I wasn't spending Christmas with the B's. I was incredibly happy at my parents' house. I had missed my mum, dad and three siblings, so I made the most of us being together. I was so glad I didn't have a complicated family. Our Christmas was peaceful and harmonious. We were so lucky.

When I returned to Nottingham on Boxing Day night, Ravi wasn't in. He had lined up a selection of Christmas cards on the side dresser. I looked at them, inspecting each one in turn. There was a humourous one from Eric and Andy, Ravi's close friends. Rob and Mia had sent one with a picture on the front of their family, all grinning, wearing Christmas jumpers and plastic antlers. Ravi had mentioned them a few times. There was Anna's glittery card, a small one from a box set from Kiko, a traditional one from Joyce and Alan next door and a cute one from someone called Nikki. It read "Love always, from your Darling Nikki." Sounds like a Prince song…who the hell is Nikki? Ravi had never mentioned that name.

Ravi walked in just as I put down the card from Nikki. "Hi, sweetheart. Sorry I'm late. I nipped out to get us a bottle of wine."

"I hope it's fizzy. I'm in the mood for bubbles."

"I got red. You like red, let's open this." He held up the bottle and it looked like a nice one, so I succumbed.

"You have some lovely cards," I pointed out, awaiting any indication of who Nikki might be.

"Yes, they're from my crowd." Ravi poured the wine.

"There's one from someone called Nikki. I don't remember you mentioning a friend by that name." Ravi stopped pouring.

"What? You've read them?" He seemed shocked. I thought he was joking and pretending to overreact. His face was solemn.

"Are you being serious?"

"Absolutely, I didn't think you'd pry into my personal things."

"They're Christmas cards, Rav, come on. lighten up. They're on display"

"Yes, they are *my* cards. You've no business reading them."

"I'm sorry, I really didn't expect you to react like this. Who *is* Nikki, anyway?"

"Are you accusing me of something? It's starting to look like you have trust issues, Georgina." He switched to his doctor/patient voice. "Have you had trust issues in the past?"

"What, no…. never. I haven't needed to doubt anyone in the past."

"Well, you're being ridiculous. Nikki is a cosmetics patient. She's been coming to me to have her face done for years. She's a sweet little old lady in her 70's."

"Jesus! People have Botox in their 70's?"

"Of course! It's for all ages. Speaking of which, your face looks like it could do with some TLC. Let's go into town and get some fizz and I'll do it for you when we get back. You can drink your bubbles while I work my magic on that face." Ravi was already putting his coat back on and I felt like a short trip out would break the tension in the house that had been created over the Nikki conversation. I felt rather foolish. Did I have trust issues? No. I didn't think so. Was I going into town for fizz, absolutely. Was I going to have Botox when we got home? Absolutely NOT!

We decided to walk into town so we could go to the local bar for one. One turned into two as we were quite enjoying the atmosphere and it physically, as well as mentally, separated us from the argument we'd had in the house. We called into the shop on the way back home and Ravi bought a bottle of my favourite sparkling wine without hesitation. He was in the good books again, but he had somehow made me feel that I had been in the wrong.

We got home, put on pyjamas and I went towards the living room sofa. We could at last relax. I was ready to chill and snuggle up with Ravi.

"Where are you going?" said Ravi as he got to the bottom of the stairs and took off his coat.

"Lounge. Wine and movie." I smiled.

"I'll get the chair ready before you get cozy. We'll do your face first. It will only take a minute; you don't need much doing."

"I don't need anything doing." I said calmly. "Let's just have a nice evening and chillax."

31

"But I've got your syringes ready in the fridge in the kitchen. I don't want them to go to waste." When did he do that? I wondered. Maybe he slipped them in when he came home?

"Well, that's your fault. You know I don't want you tampering with my face."

He laughed. "It's not tampering." He walked up to me and touched my cheek. "It will just look like you've had a good night's sleep."

"I will look like that anyway because I *am* going to get a good night's sleep tonight in bed."

I was still very calm. "I told you, I'm not having bloody Botox, so you can stick your syringes where the sun doesn't shine."

"And I thought you were so lovely. Sweet and polite."

"I am." I raised my voice. "You need to listen to me and process what I'm saying to you. I am not having needles stuck in my face. Just accept it, Ravi. It's my choice." I turned to go into the lounge, and he went to get two glasses. I believed that I had said enough to put an end to the Botox conversation once and for all.

6 OUT OUT

After the lockdown, we both returned to our normal routines. My nine to five contract along with Ravi's weekdays at the surgery and Saturdays at his aesthetics clinic made it tricky to find time together. The bubble had burst but we made it work. The time we did get together was so much more precious. However, there were times when I felt disappointed when Ravi explained that he was exceedingly busy playing catch up with patients and that many of his patients had been left in dreadful situations and needed more attention. I completely understood. These people would now be a priority and rightly so. Then one evening, he came home and said, "I've been thinking…now we're back to normal, you can move back into your house. There's no need for you to live here anymore."

I was shocked and stunned. I thought things were going really well between us. We'd been living together for a while now, happily, or so I thought. I was even beginning to think along the lines of happily ever after, 'til death do us part type scenario.

"Well, there's no reason for you to be living here now, sweetheart. Don't you miss your garden and your family? You can still leave some of your things here." I had acquired a set of drawers and a whole wardrobe for myself in Ravi's spare guest bedroom. Is he throwing me out? I wondered.

"Don't be disappointed, you can still come over on weekends. We did fall into our relationship super quickly because of lockdown. We can date again, properly. It will be fun."

Ravi had a way of selling it to me. He made the idea of dating again sound exciting and romantic. We had been living in each other's pocket basically from the word go. We had been forced into a situation that would, in normal circumstances, not have happened until a year or more into the relationship. Although to me, it seemed like we were taking a step backwards if I moved out, Ravi convinced me that it was the right move for our relationship to blossom and bloom.

"But before you go, let's do that face of yours."

He pulled the kitchen chair under the light, and I sat down. My energy was zapped, and my morale was low. It was the right time to get me under the spotlight and the needle. He went to the fridge and came back with the little box. "Look up." The transformation began.

One day at work, a colleague commented on how good I looked. I felt elated. I didn't think anyone would notice. I was wrong. I should have trusted Ravi. It's his job. He's been doing it for years and he's trained all over the world.

Ravi had told me, "You'll just look like you've had a good night's sleep. You will still look like you, don't worry, sweetheart." He was right. I felt on top of the world with my new look, my fresher, rejuvenated look. More importantly, I still looked like me. Ravi now had my trust.

I saw Ravi once a week at weekends. We were both kept busy playing catch up at work throughout the week. We would go out on Saturday evenings and I would stay over and leave on Sunday, late afternoon, in order to give us both time to get ready for work the following day. This continued for quite a few weeks, until one Saturday I arrived at the house to find no answer when I rang the doorbell. I knocked loudly, a couple of times. Still no answer. I rang Ravi's mobile. No response. It was raining so I went to sit in my car that I had parked on the front drive as usual. Just as I was contemplating driving into town to occupy myself for a while, my phone rang.

"Oh, hi, sweetheart. I'm just ringing to let you know that I am running late. I'll be there in about half an hour. I'll see you at the house."

OK, I'll wait, I thought. An hour and a half later, Ravi arrived.

"A patient was running late so I had to wait for them. She's a valued client and she travels up from London, so I had to stay on a bit longer."

"That's a long way to travel for Botox. Why doesn't she go to a clinic in London?"

"I don't charge London prices, plus she likes my work."

"Well, you are good at your job. I can see why people trust you. Plus, you're a G.P. so you know what you're doing."

"Precisely. Let's go out for dinner tonight. We'll have to sort you out with a key, so this doesn't happen again. You can let yourself in then if ever I am running late. You won't have to wait outside in the car." A small step forwards in the right direction, I smiled to myself. Ravi was right again, it felt like we were dating again. We had a perfect night out in a newly opened French bistro. We walked into the village, ate out to help out, had a gorgeous bottle of wine, then got home and had the best sex ever. Things were perfect again.

Our Saturday/Sunday arrangement continued happily and if ever Ravi was running late at work, I could let myself in now with my newly cut key and make myself at home.

One Friday night, I was invited to meet up with him and some of his friends for dinner. "I'm letting you into my friendship circle now," he said, "must be serious. You might as well stay all weekend and go home on Sunday as usual.

34

I'll be at the cosmetics clinic on Saturday, but I'm sure you can amuse yourself while I'm at work." Great, we were making progress.

I was given the name and location of the restaurant. Ravi would go straight from work, and I would go to Ravi's to get changed out of my work clothes and then get a taxi to the restaurant. When I got there, Rav was already seated at the table. I joined him and said I hoped that his friends would like me. As they arrived, Ravi introduced me to everyone in turn. Eric and Andy arrived first, shortly followed by Rob and his wife Mia. Eric and Andy were a laugh a minute. They said they'd heard all about me from Rav. All good things, but he hadn't told them how gorgeous I was. Thanks to my new face, I thought, but didn't mention the Botox.

They all, for the most part, made me feel welcome from the get-go. Mia, however, was a little suspicious and I could tell that Rob felt a little embarrassed by her questions. "So, what attracted you to Ravi?" asked Mia, her eyes narrowed. The starters arrived, so it felt an inconvenient moment to ask such a question. "Well after we matched on the dating app, we messaged for ages and we just, well, seemed to click. We had a video call before we had our first date and then lockdown hit us, so we never really looked back after that. We laugh a lot together and have a lot in common." Mia did not seem convinced and as the corners of her mouth attempted to smile, just murmured "Mmmmmm." She raised her eyebrows. What a strange reaction, I thought, but it's natural for your partner's friends to want to suss you out, right?

"How do you know Ravi?" I asked her.

"Oh, he would come to our restaurant every Friday before lockdown, and we had just gotten into a nice little Friday night routine before we had to close the trattoria. You should come and eat there one night with Ravi," she said, quite matter of fact and straight faced.

The following Friday, we all met at Mia and Rob's restaurant "Ria's" (a combo of their names), a large Italian diner type trattoria with red and green décor and rustic, chunky wooden farmhouse tables and chairs. There was gentle Italian music playing away in the background, just a soft hum so you could hear and be heard in conversation. "This is so lovely," I delighted.

"Yes, isn't it just," smiled Ravi.

"We should get back into our Friday routine," agreed Rob and Eric. As we were leaving, Eric stopped in his tracks and turned to Ravi and said, "I forgot to mention, I bumped into Nikki a couple of days ago. She's looking really good. She's lost weight. She mentioned she was having her 40th birthday party soon. Are you guys going?" I'd had a couple of glasses of red, but I remembered that Nikki was a little old lady in her 70's according to Ravi. Was this a different Nikki? I wasn't going to ruin our lovely evening and so convinced myself that there were two Nikkis. There was a sandstorm brewing in my head but the dust eventually settled, and I put it to one side. Ravi had said he was too busy to attend anyway, so there was no point in making an issue of things. Moreover, I didn't want an argument in front of Ravi's friends.

And so, I was included in Friend's Friday. Over time, I established a friendship of my own with Ravi's chums. We got on really well. Eric and Andy came over to eat with us at Rav's house every now and again. Rob and Mia were always too busy with the restaurant.

One Friday night at the trattoria, Mia and I were having a girlie chat and Mia mentioned that they had taken on a new manager at the restaurant so she and Rob could have a bit more free time together. She said that after seeing Ravi and I together and listening to our stories, she had convinced Rob that they needed to spend some quality time together, rather than constantly being at the restaurant all the time. She asked me about my Nottingham routine and was interested in knowing which days and evenings I came to stay with Ravi. I told her about our weekend routine and said that I was, more often than not, free on Saturday mornings and sometimes early afternoons as Ravi was at his cosmetics clinic. On hearing this, Mia invited me to her house. Well, I say me, but she made it crystal clear that she meant Ravi and I. So much for the girlie bonding, I thought.

"You must come round for coffee one afternoon when you are in Nottingham," she said during our tête a tête.

"Oh, lovely, that will be nice. I'm coming over next weekend as usual, so could call round on Saturday afternoon." I thought I could visit before Ravi got home from work.

"Yes, good, you and Ravi." She glanced over at Ravi, but he was in deep conversation with Rob, Eric and Andy. Ravi was talking about being interested in getting into the property business after hearing that Eric and Andy had bought a house to renovate and rent out. He was always on the lookout for new projects.

Oh, both of us. I thought she wanted to get to know me. She actually wants Ravi to go round as well. There was an awkward silence. Rav turned around, smiled at me and asked, "Alright. Sweetheart?"

"Yes, Mia has just invited us over on Saturday afternoon, but you'll be at work, won't you?"

"Yes, that's right. I won't finish until around 5pm. I've got a lot of clients booked in for Botox and fillers next week."

I was just about to say that I was happy to come over alone, have a girlie get together, female bonding and all that when…

"Come over on Saturday night then, when you get in from work…" she slid in like a snake. I was not amused. She knew that Ravi and I always had our date night on Saturdays, dining out or a cozy movie and takeaway, whatever, but an intimate evening together – alone.

Please say no, please say no, please say no. But Ravi, as polite as ever, said, "That's kind of you, Mia. What time would you like us to come over?"

And so, it began, a tiny crack appeared. Date night Saturday was spent with Mia the following week. No sign of Rob. He was away on business, Mia informed us. Great! Just the three of us. We were there to keep Mia company, and she had got in the way of our romantic date night. I found it really difficult to relax that night. Mia kept plying Ravi with wine, but my drink wasn't going down so easily. Mia enjoyed reminding us all that she had known Ravi longer than I had and that their daughters were good friends. It's not a competition, I thought. I'm not a jealous natured soul, but I could feel my blood simmering. This woman was no friend of mine, but I knew I would have to politely tolerate her and play the good girlfriend role for Ravi's sake. The evening dragged for me, and I couldn't wait to get home and snuggle up with my man. Finally, Ravi announced that it was late, and that we should be going. Yay! But Mia tried the one last drink trick, and it worked. When we did get home, Ravi said he was going straight to bed to sleep as he was feeling more than drowsy. I stayed up a while, I was angry with Mia. She had sabotaged our Saturday and Ravi had allowed it to happen. The following morning Ravi was sound asleep or should I say unconscious. He was out for the count until midday. When he eventually came downstairs, he was not in great shape.

"I'm so hungover. I can't remember the last time I felt like this."

"Well, I'll be honest with you. I've had better Saturday nights."

"Did you not have a good time, sweetheart?"

"Well, it was OK to begin with but then Mia just got blind drunk and then you seemed to follow suit."

"Oh, did I? I don't really remember that much about last night."

"Exactly, you got so drunk, the conversation completely disintegrated, and I just wanted to come home. Plus, Saturday is our night together."

"Are you saying we shouldn't be seeing our friends? I've known Mia for ages."

"No, that's absolutely not what I'm saying. At one point it turned into the Mia monologues, and I'd had enough. How many issues does she have? Is she a hypochondriac? I think she would like you to be her private personal doctor and counsellor."

I tried to explain my point of view, but Ravi said I was being melodramatic and insecure. I disagreed. My spider sense was not usually wrong. We agreed not to discuss it any further as we now only had what was left of Sunday and the cherry on the cake, Ravi had a headache.

That night in bed, Ravi concluded that after giving it some thought, he agreed with me. Saturday was our date night and that either I should have gone over to Mia's on my own earlier while he was at work, or he should have suggested a different evening. I was glad he spoke the words but verbalizing it now was too late. Saturday had happened. It was in the past, but it was also in the captain's log. Star date 2020 – Don't trust Mia!

"If she asks again, I'll say no as you don't feel comfortable going round. I'll just go on my own." I didn't rise to this, there was potential for a mighty storm. I'm not an argumentative person, so I let it go. Ravi seemed to have a positive versus negative narrative at times. I put it down to his busy work routine. I often caught him walking round the living room, chuntering out loud. When I had mentioned it to mum, she'd said that dad was just the same. They are scientists and busy people. I've always said that your father has a butterfly mind. He flits from one thought to another, and you can't get caught up in it or you'll go crazy. Mmmm maybe that was the downfall of the exes. Perhaps that's what drove them mad.

The next time Ravi and I met up with the gang, Eric brought Nikki back into conversation. "You missed a great night last night, you guys. You should have come; you were both invited. Nikki's moved on and so have you, Rav." Andy turned towards me, "I can understand you not wanting to be at Ravi's ex's party though, Georgie. A bit weird for you."

Ravi cut in sharply. "I wanted to take Georgie out last night, just the two of us. We had a lovely evening, didn't we, sweetheart?"

"Yes, lovely." I hid my disdain and shame about not being aware that Nikki was an ex. But then again, why was I not surprised! I was blind sided in that instant and angry at Ravi for not having told the truth. Another lie. I would tackle that later with Ravi once we were in the privacy of his home.

There was a stifled atmosphere throughout the rest of the evening and Mia kept asking me if I was alright. "I'm just tired," I feigned. "Ravi and I were out late last night."

"He was out really late on Tuesday as well when he came round here," said Mia with a grin on her face. "He got so drunk! At one point he fell on me, and we could hardly get up."

"You didn't tell me you'd been round to Mia's this week, Rav." I tried to sound casual, but smoke was oozing from the volcano.

"No? She wanted me to do her face. She's impressed with the work I've done on yours and asked if I'd come round and work my miracles."

"I cooked him a lovely dinner," added Mia with glee, "…to thank him. I brought a bottle or two of Prosecco from the bar at Ria's and we ended up finishing the lot."

Rob chipped in, "Yes, she never cooks for me when I'm at home."

"You always eat at the ristorante, Rob, or bring the leftovers home, so I never need to cook."

"Mia cooked all my favourites," smiled Ravi. "Arancini with tomato sauce, then a gorgeous mushroom risotto, followed by tiramisu. Food fit for a king!"

He looked at Mia and as they shared a smile, the molten lava in the pit of my stomach began to stir. Did she now? That was jolly nice of her! How I managed to keep my lid on, I don't know.

When Ravi and I got in that night we did not see eye to eye. To say that we had a difference of opinion is an understatement. I pointed out that Mia was jealous of our relationship and that whenever Rob was away on business, she always wanted Ravi to go round and keep her company. She was not interested in being my friend or spending time with me unless Ravi was there. I explained that it was not healthy for our relationship for Ravi to visit Mia on her own, get drunk and fall on top of her. The fact was that Mia was available during the week now, Ravi found time to see her, Rob went away a lot and there was potential for an affair. Now I felt paranoid!

"She always wants to see you on your own, without me, when Rob's away. Can't you see what she's doing? She's coming between us and you're letting her." I was so frustrated.

"There's nothing like that between us; we are very good friends. You have friends, don't you? You'll be telling me not to go round to Mia's soon and deciding who I can and can't see. If you can't get on with Mia, maybe you should stop coming out with us on Fridays. You really should see someone about your trust issues." Ravi seemed genuinely concerned.

Even though I was 100% sure that Mia was up to no good, I had to regain Ravi's faith in me. I had caused him to doubt me, which was not my intention. I had wanted him to see and understand my point of view and empathise with me. I felt let down, but I knew how lucky I was to have Ravi as my partner and did not want to risk losing him. I raised the white flag and decided to make peace with Mia.

During that week, I happened to bump into a good friend of mine at the gym. I had kept my own circle of friends through the thick and thin of lockdown. I had known Helen since junior school. She was now a psychologist. We were waiting for Zumba to start. The instructor was running late as usual, so we had time to touch base. I trusted Helen. "I have something to ask you, H."

"Sounds serious," she replied. "Is everything OK?"

"Do you think I have trust issues?"

"You? Trust issues? No. You are the person least likely to have trust issues. You take things at face value, weigh up situations and are usually right with the conclusions that you draw. I know you, you're sound, G. Why are you asking?"

"Well, I'm not sure if I'm losing my marbles, going mad, or the perimenopause is kicking in, but something's off. I've been suspicious of Ravi. Nothing concrete that I can put my finger on, but something's not right. I can't figure out if I'm self-sabotaging or going insane."

"As long as I've known you, you've always been of sound mind…maybe a bit wild at times, but completely sane."

"Ravi is convinced I have trust issues. Whenever I try to talk to him about certain situations, he tries to make out that I'm insecure. He won't discuss things properly. I've noticed that he is a master of changing the subject, or worse, he makes me feel like I'm in the wrong when I say I'm not happy with his behaviour."

"Oh, my God, G, he's gaslighting you! Trust your gut, Georgie."

The instructor had arrived and set up her music while we were in deep discussion. I looked at her and nodded. I just had enough time to nod at Helen and thank her. I couldn't wait to get home and look up the meaning of 'gaslighting'. I had a vague idea but wasn't sure.

The instructor shouted out "Hi" to everyone and then let out a mighty roar "Zumbaaaaaaa..." At the end of the class Helen told me to remember what she had said. "Trust your instinct. Take care, I have to rush back home for the kids."

So now I was on guard. I was beginning to find it difficult to separate fact from fiction, truth from lies. Even my own face had become a deception, an illusion, an alternative reality. I was happy for the most part, but the mirror was starting to crack. The honeymoon period was over. How would we battle the obstacles?

Ravi's birthday was approaching, and I wanted to plan a surprise party. It would be a small affair, away from Ria's. I would choose somewhere local and low key. It would be cute and fun, like we had been together when we first met. We would get back on track and move on from the mess that I had created. I would invite Rav's closest friends, have a cake made, pre-order and pay for all the food, so no one could offer to pay and take over. There would be balloons and streamers and banners and I would create a magical wonderland for my gorgeous boyfriend. He treated me like a princess. I would show my appreciation and love for him by throwing the best party ever.

The following Friday night at Ria's I gave out handmade invitations to Eric and Andy, Mia and Rob, while Rav went to use the bathroom. I quickly told them not to say anything to Ravi, as it was a secret surprise party. All the details regarding time, venue etc. were in the card. They managed to hide the cards away in time for Ravi's return to the table and he was none the wiser. Later on, when I went to the toilet, Mia came into the bathroom seconds later.

"Are you inviting Anna and Kiko?" she asked.

"I don't really know them and as we haven't met yet, I don't have their contact information."

"I'll ask my daughter for Anna's number and send it to you so you can invite them. They should be there; Ravi will love it."

I thanked Mia for her help, and she said if there was anything else she could do, I should just ask. She was thankful to Ravi for doing her face and wanted to contribute. She even offered to provide the desserts from Ria's. I said that I had everything in hand, but it was a good idea of hers to get Rav's children to come. Mia and I were finally bonding.

I found the perfect venue. The lady that owned and ran it gave me free reign to create a Spanish type menu, and she was very kind about the price. She offered to bake the birthday cake as well, which was great. That way I would only need to buy the candles and arrange for the cake to be brought out after our main course tapas style buffet. I bought balloons on the Saturday morning of the party and took them to the restaurant while Rav was at work. I left glitter for the table and banners so the staff could decorate the table ready for the soirée. Everything was ready and Ravi had no idea. When he got home that afternoon, I wished him a happy birthday and presented him with a box. I told him that he would have to wait until later as I'd booked us a table in town for cocktails and tapas and the taxi was on its way.

When we got to the restaurant all the gang, including Anna were there. Kiko had declined the invitation, saying that he had already arranged to go away with friends. Our little corner of the room was decorated with the usual party decorations plus the personal touches that I had brought. It all looked lovely and when Ravi walked in everyone shouted, "Happy Birthday Ravi!"

He was astounded. He was speechless. After a moment when he'd had a chance to take it all in, he turned to me and asked, "When did you organise all this, sweetheart? This is amazing. Anna, you're here. Amazing. Georgie you're so wonderful!" I was so pleased that everything had gone so smoothly. We were all laughing, joking and sharing stories. Ravi wanted to know every detail of how I'd put the party together without his knowledge. I got to know Anna and she said she'd had an idea about me because; "Dad has not been coming over for food all the time like he used to and Kiko mentioned that he had seen dad with a woman, shopping in the supermarket."

Everything was perfect again. Everyone was happy and getting along. The birthday boy was loving every minute, and I felt content. I leant over and whispered in Rav's ear, "You still have your present to open when we get home." Ravi kissed me and we clinked our glasses together. "Cheers." I said, looking into his eyes. The others all shouted in unison, "Cheers, Ravi. Happy Birthday!"

Then Anna's lone voice added, "Cheers dad, Happy 60th."

It was my turn to be astounded. The chatting and laughter of the party continued while I slipped into a parallel universe of blurry slow motion. It was as if I was under water, not drowning, but unable to speak or make anything out clearly. Who the hell had I arranged a party for? I didn't know this man. We had agreed on honesty and openness. I suddenly felt like a stranger. I looked at everyone around me, having a lovely time. I was not going to spoil it, but boy oh boy, Birthday Boy, you have some explaining to do. The cake came out, candles and all. Luckily I hadn't gone for any numerical party decorations. Imagine my embarrassment if I'd have gone for a 55 on the cake...or the balloons. Did everyone know Ravi's age? Was I the only one not in the loop? The party came to a natural conclusion when the staff started to clear some of the surrounding tables. I had put on my smiley party face throughout, but I wasn't feeling in the party mood since Anna's revelation. The gang all offered to pay their way, but I smugly announced that everything had been taken care of. Mia tried to insist on contributing, but it was all done and dusted.

We were about to leave, and everyone was ready for home when Mia offered her house up as a venue for carrying on the party. I knew it was too good to be true, she's after the limelight again. Why on earth could she not just go home and let Ravi and I have the rest of the night together. Ravi said he would be up for it if everyone agreed, but Anna declined, saying she had work to do on

Sunday and Eric and Andy said they were calling it a night. I thanked them for coming and they left. Mia then tried to persuade Ravi to "party on". I put my foot down and looked Mia right in the eyes and said that I'd got something else in mind at home for Ravi and I. "I know exactly what you're going to say, sweetheart." Ravi giggled with drunken buffoonery.

"Well, why don't you start then?" I said angrily.

"If I'd have put on my profile that my name was Ravindra, I was 59 years of age and five foot six would you have swiped left or right?"

"Erm…" I hesitated. "I did like your pictures, but if I'm honest, I think the age and height would have put me off."   "So, you'd have swiped left?"

"Yes, I believe so."

"And do you think we are a good match now that you know me?"   "Yes, but…I'm not sure who you actually are at times…"

"I knew no one would believe me if I put my real age because of the cosmetic work I've had done. My looks and my age don't match. You women all want someone tall, dark and handsome, so I had to lie about my height. You all want to be able to wear heels." He continued, "You all want the perfect man. We don't get that many matches as you women on these sites. Men are not as picky as women."

Once again, Ravi was right. I could see his point of view. I felt sorry for him, looking at him in a state of inebriated patheticism, trying to justify why he'd lied. I pitied him, having had to create a false persona to attract women. I did understand and I did still love him.

"OK, but what about Nikki, your little 70-year-old patient ex-girlfriend who's recently had her 40th birthday party and is looking good?"

"There you go again. I know how jealous and possessive you can be, so I played it down about Nikki. She's not for me, you are, sweetheart." Ravi moved towards me, and I let him hug me, while I just stood, processing everything, trying to figure out how I felt about it all." Helen's words rang in my head, "Trust your instinct." I believed what Ravi had said, and it all seemed feasible. It was a lot, but I could accept what he had said and move forwards. Keep calm and carry on.

So, onwards we continued. Life is never perfect, but it had certainly been more complicated than I was used to during the last couple of years or so.

You ride the bumps, overcome the obstacles and celebrate the positives in a relationship. I was still happy with Ravi, although I began to sense that our partnership was becoming rather one-sided. Life carried on and things began to further develop family wise. Anna and Kiko came round for coffee or drinks and food every once in a while. Fun Friday carried on in pretty much the same way. Ravi came to my parents' for Christmas 2021 and my whole family fell in love with him. Mum in particular said how charming and gorgeous he was. I think my sister had a secret crush. Of course, he had given me some money to go out and choose presents for each one of them, saying that as he didn't know them, this would be the best plan. We all went out for pre-Christmas dinner drinks at our local pub and Ravi was the centre of attention. He chatted with strangers at the bar, staff working tirelessly to clear tables and drinks, and even offered to help clear up. A few of the neighbours called in and Ravi instantly enchanted them with his magic spell. Abracadabra! Everyone was hooked. Captain's log. Star date 2021 – Everybody loves Ravi!

We had planned to spend Boxing Day at Anna's. Kiko would join us later with his new girlfriend. Ravi dropped me off at the house while he went to the clinic. He had promised Anna a Botox touch up and had left the syringes at work. Ravi drove straight off, and I was just putting the key in the front door when Joyce appeared from nowhere.

"Merry Christmas, Georgie! Did you get our card?"

"No, we've been in Holmfirth with my family. But thank you. Merry Christmas!"

As I got through the front door, there was a pile of cards on the floor. I picked them up, remembering that Ravi did not like me opening his cards, but you know what, I thought to hell with it. That was last year. We were so much closer now. There were the usual cards from the gang. Nikki had sent one, no stamp, so I assumed she had delivered it by hand. That got ripped up and went straight into the bin. Out of sight, out of mind. There was one from Joyce and Alan next door. It read, "Have a lovely Christmas wherever you may be!" What did that mean? Ravi is always at work, and when he's not at work, he's at home. Surely Joyce and Alan would notice his car on the drive every night. Wherever would he be? I didn't keep tabs on Ravi, I knew his routine was basically work, sometimes gym, then home. He never stayed out. If he met up with friends, he was always home by 10pm ready for surgery the following day. There were a couple of times when he'd gone over to Mia's to do her face, but he would always stay at home. Something triggered my spider sense. As Ravi pulled the car onto the drive, Joyce was outside adjusting her pleached fig tree.

"Thank you for the card, Joyce. I guess you can't keep track of my comings and goings to and from Ravi's house. It's difficult knowing when I'm here."

"We usually know when *you're* here, Georgina. We see your car every weekend and sometimes in the week. It's Ravi we can't keep track of. He's never here." She smiled at me, kindly. It was a kind of sympathetic knowing smile. There was meaning behind it. It was full of good intention, almost protective and caring towards me. Joyce was trying to tell me something, without directly interfering. I got into Ravi's car and as we sped off, he said, "I didn't know you were so chatty with the neighbours. What do you talk about?" He was curiously on edge, which puzzled me, as it was a very natural thing to do. I liked Joyce, she was always very chirpy, upbeat and very knowledgeable about plants. She was straight forward, honest and open. I think that's why we got along so well.

"Joyce and I have gardening in common and we often talk over the wall in the back garden when the weather's nice, usually about gardening, and what we are both growing, how unkempt my own garden is…Just chit chat, you know? You got a Christmas card from them."

"Oh, that's nice, sweetheart. I bet you opened it, didn't you?"

"While you were at the clinic, yes. It's a bit odd though, as it says '…wherever you may be'…"

"Yes, that is odd. She probably just means that we're always out socialising."

But we weren't always out socialising. At least, I wasn't always out. I was at work during the week, then either at the gym or at home planning lessons and marking. Only occasionally did I come through to Nottingham on a school night.

"She's never liked me. Not since I moved in. She never talks to me. I think she enjoys spying on me because she has nothing better to do." This was not the impression of Joyce that I had. She always said hello to us both in passing. I couldn't imagine her ignoring Rav when I wasn't there. It didn't make sense. Joyce was always very friendly and always said hello to people.

I logged the Joyce situation and kept it on the back burner. Too many issues had been registered and stored in my archive file, so I tried to put them all behind me and focus on the positives. I did not, however, permanently delete them. A few weeks later, Ravi announced that it would be good for us to get away.

"You book the holiday and plan the activities. You are good at doing that. Use your card and I'll give you the cash." I was happy with that. I loved researching new places, finding out about what there was of interest, organising activities and experiencing new things. We agreed that it was too soon to be planning a holiday abroad given the current climate.

My parents had taken us to Devon when my siblings and I were toddlers. I had zero recollection of these many holidays spent down South. I had an old photograph of me on a beach, eating ice cream, sun-kissed and grinning. Possibly about four years old. I had always had an urge to go back. Paul said he had never been to Devon. "What, never?" I was surprised. "I thought you'd been everywhere."

"I've travelled all over the world, Australia, Dubai, Europe, Asia…. but never Devon. Devon it is, then, we both agreed.

We had an absolutely amazing holiday in Devon. It was fantastic. I had booked a great hotel in Okehampton with falconry on site, pony trekking in Dartmoor National Park, a train ride from Launceston through beautiful scenic landscapes and a bicycle trip in the heart of the countryside. We took a thousand photographs to record our happiness and upon our return home, I had some framed and placed around both our houses: mantlepieces, bedroom side tables, dining room dresser. Happy, in love and looking forward to a bright future, the next step was a holiday a bit further afield.
"What about Ireland?" I suggested.

"Yes, Ireland's nice, I've been a few times."

"Oh, so not Ireland, then."

"I'm happy to go again. Each time I've gone it has been different and once it was for work…a conference, so that was boring. I've also been with Mel, but as she was a big drinker, she was usually very drunk and rowdy, and I didn't enjoy it much. All we did was pub crawls and tours involving alcohol."

"OK, let's do Ireland. I'll make sure it's lots of fun and you'll have a really great time. It will be fab. No work, no drunkenness, just fun and culture."

So, Ireland was a hoot, we visited the Cliffs of Moher and Galway on a coach trip, spent evenings listening to live folk music. It was fun from start to finish. We were on a roll. We saw the Book of Kells, had a day trip to the Giant's

Causeway, and had coffee in the Irish Museum of Modern Art.

We were both keen to book somewhere abroad. It had been three years. Two years basically in lockdown and if not some kind of restrictions, testing, Covid passporting and one year when things were calming down, feeling rather unsure and uncertain about booking a holiday at all for fear of any more Covid issues.

Enough time had elapsed, and we decided to just go for it. We were both itching to travel abroad. We, or rather I, booked with all the Covid insurance in existence to make sure that we were covered from all angles, should anything virus-linked befall either of us. Ravi had missed his cruises. We had been to Devon and Ireland, and I had enjoyed every minute of both trips. They had been fun, adventurous and just simply wonderful. I had never been on a cruise. I was not interested in going on a cruise, I was not a great lover of the sea, being at sea, nor spending time overnight on a ship in the sea. But now I was in a relationship. Two people to think of. It was not all about me. Ravi had been more than generous, paying for the holidays, giving me free reign to book activities and choose restaurants. I would get over myself and my pre-conceived ideas of cruise life and do it. He loved cruises. How bad could they be? I would learn to love cruises too.

A few days later, Ravi reminded me that he had always wanted to go to the Amalfi Coast. "Oh my god, me too, yes, that's somewhere else you have never been?"

"No, and it's on my bucket list so do you want to investigate that. I fancy a road trip."

"How come you've been everywhere and not visited that part of Italy?"

"Well, I just haven't. No reason"

"I would absolutely love to go. It's supposed to be beautiful there…. But we've already booked the cruise. Yes, but the cruise is for Easter, and I was thinking we could do say ten days in the Summer."

"Absolutely!" I was ecstatic. "But you must let me pay this time."

"I'll tell you what, I'll pay for the travel and accommodation. You can pay for the activities you choose to book, if you like?"

"Well, that's more than fair, Thank you. You are so good to me." I flung my arms around him, and he smiled humbly. I hunted out the scrap book and set to work.

So that was Easter and Summer sorted! We had two great holidays to look forward to and life was sweet – just as I liked it.

7 IS THERE ANYBODY OUT THERE?

One night when Rav was in the shower, his landline rang. I wondered whether I should answer it, but by the time I had decided to do so, it rang off. Seconds later it rang again, so I said, "Hello," as I picked up the receiver, but the phone immediately went dead. When Ravi came out of the bathroom, I told him he'd missed a call (but I didn't mention that I'd picked up). At the time, I didn't think to try ring back or dial to acquire the last telephone number. It just triggered a small alarm bell.

"I never use the landline," Ravi said. "Just ignore it if it rings again, it will only ever be a cold call."

On another occasion, I arrived on Friday evening and rang Rav to say that I was running late and would get to the trattoria about half an hour after him. There was no answer, so I assumed that he was busy with work. When I mentioned this at the ristorante, Ravi said he had left his phone at the house that morning. Unusual, I thought, he never does that. He needs it to take important calls. Plus, I didn't hear it ringing in the house while I was getting ready at Ravi's earlier. He's always got his phone in his coat pocket. He never goes anywhere without it. Actually, he rarely gets his phone out when he's with me, which is a good thing as that way he gives me his full attention. I pondered a while on how secretive Ravi was with his mobile, but didn't give it any serious thought at the time.

The following Friday, I arrived at the house and as I pulled up on the drive and got out of the car, I said hi to Joyce. She was pruning her fig tree, and I was immediately interested about how she got her fruit to be so big and healthy. She had previously expressed her joy at Ravi, "having found someone nice at last." But what she said to me just before I let myself into the house was, to my mind, more than small talk. "It's nice to see you, Georgie. We haven't seen either of you all week. I never know when Ravi's around. Ravi's car is never there and when it is, he's gone in a flash. He's like a ghost. He only seems to live here when you come over." I laughed rather awkwardly and said, "Well, we live in two separate houses so I guess you can expect a lot of coming and going. Ravi has a very busy work schedule." I wanted to escape into the house and process what she had said. Hindsight is a wonderful thing and if I could turn back time,

I would have quizzed her more on Ravi's "comings and goings". I walked past the landline phone as I got in the house. I decided to use it to ring my phone. That way, I would have Ravi's landline number. I just thought it might be useful if ever he didn't answer his mobile. I didn't believe that he never used it. Otherwise, why would he still have it?

The following Thursday, at my house, I called Ravi. There was no answer. We met as usual on Friday for dinner at Ria's, but I did not mention to Rav that I had tried to call. The weekend went by without anything unusual.

During the week, I called Ravi…on Thursday. There was no answer again. I got a message on Friday lunchtime. "Hi, sweetheart. I'm going to be late tonight. Go ahead and order and I'll join you when I can." That night I made sure to get there early. I casually spoke with Rob, Andy and Eric. Mia brought us drinks and said that Ravi was running late. Odd! How does Mia know? Anyway, I needed to speak with the guys before Ravi arrived. "I ring Ravi out of work hours, and he sometimes doesn't answer, do you think that's strange?"

"Oh, he's probably just busy," said Andy.

"Yes but it's always on a Thursday night and I can never get through. Sometimes his phone is even switched off." There was an awkward, uncomfortable silence. Eric and Andy looked at each other. They reported to have zero information, but their reaction triggered my spider sense.

"I would talk to him about it," they agreed. And that's basically all they had to say on the matter.

"Well, let's have a nice dinner, and I'll have a chat with him later." Ravi arrived and we spent another pleasant chatty evening over pasta and Prosecco.

When we got back to the house, trying my best to be casual about the whole thing, I did ask Ravi, "I tried ringing you last night and you're phone was switched off. I know this probably sounds like an odd question, but if you were seeing someone else, would you tell me? I would like to think that I could walk away, no questions asked, we are still in the relatively early stages of our relationship…If you want to see other women, that's fine, but I don't want a complicated situation. I left my life in France because it just got too complicated. I really don't want to re-live the same scenario."

"You know how busy I am, sweetheart. I had a really stressful day yesterday and when I got home, I just wanted to relax, without any interruptions. I switched my phone off so I wouldn't get disturbed. I just wanted some peace and quiet." I felt divided. Again, as always, Ravi made a good point. It seemed reasonable and I was now doubting my spider sense. I was so sure that there was something going on, but maybe I was being oversensitive?

"*Have* you had trust issues in the past, sweetheart? I can put you in touch with someone if you want." said Ravi in a calm, cool, unfaltering manner. Here we go again. Ravi was deflecting.

"No, definitely not," I affirmed. "I've never had trust issues. I can just sense when something is off."

"Well, it sounds to me like you are having trust issues. A relationship is built around trust and if we can't trust each other, then it's not a great foundation." I hesitated, disappointed in myself and the fact that he was right about what makes for a strong foundation in a relationship. Of course, we had to trust each other. What was I thinking. I had let him down even thinking that he could be having an affair. Give up this ridiculous idea. I had probably lost part of my sanity during the Covid lockdown and lost touch with reality. Ravi was lovely…. perfect in fact. We'd had fantastic holidays, weekends were going well, Mia, for the most part was in the background. I was not going to sabotage my wonderful relationship because I was having a moment of self-doubt. I would forget about any flight of fancy I was experiencing and focus on the reality of the situation. The cold hard facts. The evidence. I am a clear-headed individual. I have a logical mind. I was being ridiculous. It was all speculation, and I had created silly stories in my head. Just because he hadn't answered his phone a couple of times.   I   would   let   it   lay.

8 THE TRUTH WILL OUT

However, I could not let it lay. It was there, stuck in my head, like a small seed, planted, present and biding its time. Not growing, just sitting, awaiting germination. How to resolve this? I had to attend to it. If I water the seeds in my greenhouse, with heat and light they grow. If I leave them unattended, they rot, and I lose any hope of an actual plant forming. I would approach the matter carefully and think things through, step by step. The situation: I suspect Ravi is not telling the truth, at least about Thursday nights. His phone is often switched off. If it rings, he does not answer and if I call again, the only response I get is from an automated answering machine…or he switches off his device. His friends went uncomfortably quiet when I brought up the subject at Ria's and they definitely looked at one another and had a mutual "knowing" look. When I broached the subject with Ravi, he basically, more or less, no, outright, literally, accused me of having trust issues again. So, either I have trust issues (which Helen and I do not believe for one minute), and I need to arrange some form of counselling or therapy, or Ravi is in actual fact gas lighting me. How to find out? I had a key! Lightbulb moment. I would go over to Ravi's after work under the pretext of surprising him, spontaneously. What's wrong with a girlfriend dropping by to see her boyfriend unannounced? Then I'll know for sure. I felt exceedingly nervous driving down the motorway after work, wondering how Ravi would perceive my unannounced landing. After a trouble-free journey, I parked the car on the empty drive, crept to the front door and let myself in. "Ravi", I shouted, "Ravi," slightly louder. No answer. No one home. I waited an hour or so, read my book, watched the TV. He's late, I thought, two hours later. Probably busy, or at the gym. I'll see what's in the fridge and rustle up some tea. Another hour passed. I ate alone. I tried ringing. No answer. I waited until 10.30pm and decided to call it a night. Ravi had maybe gone out with friends after work and was getting back late. I went to bed, feeling sure that Ravi would arrive at some point and snuggle into bed next to me, saying, "That's a lovely surprise, I wasn't expecting you…" I fell asleep. When my alarm went off the next morning to get up for work, there was no sign of Ravi. He had not come home. I got ready for work; had a shower, got dressed, came downstairs and made a coffee for the road. When I arrived at work, I rang Ravi's phone, and it was still switched off. I got on with my day and as it was Friday, I was due to meet Ravi back at the house and then we would go to the restaurant together to meet the gang as usual. I arrived at the house first. I quickly dashed round and checked the house to see if there were any signs of Ravi having been home at all. The house was exactly as I had left it. Pristine. I could feel my heart beating in my chest, preparing what I would say when Ravi walked through the front door. I would get ready calmly, have a shower, wear a knockout dress and act naturally. I would be carefree and casual, as though nothing had happened. I would gauge the evening and how things went and somehow weave in my secret interrogation so as to go under the radar. I felt anxious as I heard Ravi turning his key in the front door. "Hi, sweetheart," he called. He had obviously seen the car parked on the drive. "Hi," I called. "I'm just getting ready…be there in a tick." As I emerged from the bedroom, he was wandering from the living room with his phone in his hand, looking at the screen. When he saw me he quickly shoved the phone into his back pocket.

"Is that what you're wearing tonight?" He asked with a rather dismissive tone.

"Absolutely, isn't it gorgeous?"

"What, you are actually going out like that?" I felt a change in his tone. It was condescending and unapproving. Had the person on the other end of the phone pissed him off? Why was he being moody? Did he know I had spent the previous night checking out whether he was telling the truth about his 'Thursday evening early night'? Ravi was evidently in a bad frame of mind, and I linked it with his secret phone communication, due to the fact that he had sounded quite cheery when he walked through the front door. As we pulled off the drive, on our way to Ria's, or so I thought, Ravi took a turn down a street in the opposite direction of the restaurant.

"Where are you going?" I wondered if he had gone into autopilot to Mia's house.

"Eric and Andy rang earlier, and they are waiting for us at a new Greek place they want to try. Sorry, I forgot to mention it, sweetheart, I've been really busy at work this week."

"That will make a nice change," I smiled. "Is it just the four of us."

"Yes, Mia has to be at her restaurant as she's short-staffed tonight and Rob is away again." Mmmm so was Ravi seeing Mia? Was he angry because he wouldn't see her tonight? Or was there something else that had happened before his phone slid away into his pocket, never to be seen again that evening. I had several possible scenarios in my head, but I felt like I was slowly creeping towards the truth. I knew Ravi was up to something. But what? We arrived at the Greek place and the guys had ordered a bottle of red wine.

"Mmmm. I was ready for this!" I sighed as I drank my first sip. "I've had a really busy week." Little did the three of them know exactly how busy! I must admit, I did get a tiny kick from being in the know. After all, knowledge is power.

"How's your week been, Ravi?" asked Andy.

"The usual nonsense. Patients are never happy, and the aesthetic side of things is busier than ever."

"I don't know where you get your energy from to do six days a week and find time to socialise," said Eric.

"Well, work hard, play hard. That's the motto, isn't it?" replied Ravi.

"Exactly," I agreed. "You do get some down time though, don't you?. Did you have an early night last night ready for this evening, so you wouldn't feel too tired?" To me, this question felt forced, rather like a pursuit of enquiry, but no one seemed to pick up on it.

"Yes," Ravi said confidently. "I started to watch a movie when I got in, but before I knew it, I had fallen asleep on the sofa."

"Oh, no, poor you." I felt zero pity. "You spent the night on the couch?"

"No, I woke up the middle of the night and got into bed."

I don't remember you being there, I thought to myself. I would swear on those near and dear to me that I was alone in the house, your house, all night. I had caught him out. I did not have trust issues. He was gaslighting me. He was so calm and straight faced as he told his version of last night. I couldn't resist. "Which film did you watch?"

"Oh, I, erm, I didn't watch it all, like I said, I fell asleep."

"You must remember what it was called at least, or who was in it...anyone famous?" Careful, G, he'll wonder why you are giving him the third degree about a movie.

"It was that one that we started to watch at the weekend...what was it called?"

"Why would you watch that one? We decided to call it a night after about 20 minutes because it bored us to tears."

"Well, I thought I'd give it another go, see if it got any better further into it."

I made a joke out of it and laughed, "Well obviously not if you fell asleep, ha ha ha..." Everyone laughed and I relaxed again. Be careful, don't be too inquisitive, G. Remember, calm, casual, fun-loving Georgie.

So, Ravi was outright lying. I did not have trust issues. Charming Ravi had the cool, calm collected skill of a master liar and deceptionist. I was stunned. I knew this for sure. But why? Was he seeing another woman? Another man? Could something else more sinister be going on? Why would he lie if it was honest and above board? I was intrigued now and felt the need to collect more evidence. Was he seeing one of his exes? Perhaps he had a secret family. You hear about these things. It was clear that he wasn't going to spill the beans. I needed to extend my plan. The following week I carried out the same experiment. Sure enough, Ravi did not come home on Thursday evening. I spent the night alone in his bed. I had not bothered to ring this time. I still had the "spontaneous surprise" story ready in my head, just in case he came home.

He did not. I went to work on the Friday morning and returned to Ravi's later that day. I got ready to go out and we set off to Ria's.

"How are you feeling?" I asked as we pulled into the restaurant car park.

"I'm fine, sweetheart. Are you OK?"

"I'm great. It's just that you look really tired tonight. You look like you haven't had any sleep." Ravi looked panicked and I could not understand why he would be so perturbed at my comment.

"Tired? No, I don't." He checked himself in the rear-view mirror, looked at me and asked, "You think I look tired?"

"Yes, I'm a bit concerned. You're not overdoing it, are you? Did you not get much sleep last night?"

"I had an early night, sweetheart. I was rather tired last night, so I watched the match and went straight to bed…I don't think I look tired." He looked in the mirror again. I realised that I had hit a nerve saying that he looked less than perfect. Who's bed? I wondered. When we got to the trattoria, Mia and Rob were sitting inside at a table in the middle of the restaurant. "Eric and Andy not here yet?" Ravi asked.

"No, they can't make it tonight, they have to baby sit." Time for a little chat with Mia and gauge Rob's reaction. Now we have two of the suspected players pinned down and no distractions. I had my investigation head on.

"So, how are you two?" I asked, unassumingly.

"We're fine, Georgina," replied Mia. "Rob got back from Hong Kong last night and I had to pick him up from the airport, but we're OK. We had a lay in this morning before coming to the restaurant mid-morning for the lunchtime crowd."

So, Ravi couldn't have been at Mia's or with Mia last night. Rob is sitting right there in plain sight, a little jet lagged, but there's Mia's alibi. Alibi! Who do I think I am? I could get into this detective lark, it's quite interesting, forming strategies and testing theories. Ravi thinks he's so clever, but maybe he's met his match.

"What have you been up to, Ravi, while I've been negotiating business deals in Hong Kong?" asked Rob.

"Not a lot, the usual, you know."

"Ravi has been so tired recently," I interjected, "look at his poor little tired face," and I pinched his check.

"I don't look tired. I told you, I'm fine," he snapped.

"Why so grumpy, Ravi?" asked Mia.

"I'm not tired or grumpy. I've just been really busy recently."

"You had time to chill last night, though, didn't you? You relaxed a bit and watched the match," I smiled, trying my best to sound natural.

"Oh, I just managed to get home in time to see it. What did you think?" Rob asked enthusiastically. This was the first football conversation I recall ever being interested in. This should be good, I thought.

"Me?" asked Ravi, startled.

"Well, he's not asking Me or Georgie," Mia laughed.

"That's very sexist, Mia," I pretended to be offended, then laughed along with her, "but true." There was a pause and the three of us looked at Ravi. At this point, I felt that I could probably trust Ria. They were not involved in the Thursday night mystery after all.

"Erm, oh the usual, I've forgotten already."

"Forgotten?" shrieked Rob, "What about those two goals?"

"Oh, er, yes, I remember those." Ravi stammered. "One match is pretty much like another to me. I was tired and had an early night. I think I must have fallen asleep at some point. I must have missed the height of the action."

Captain's log. Star date 2022- Ravi is cracking under pressure. Mia is not a threat.

"I said you looked tired." Ravi glared at me. I'd found his Achilles' heel. I glared back, knowing that he had lied to me constantly over the last two weeks. I asked Rob about Hong Kong, and he told me that he used to live there and had properties that still needed attending to. Sounds like big business, I thought. Was it possible that Ravi was wheeling and dealing abroad? How did he come to have so much cash in the house? He had told me when we first met that he was semi-retired, but yet he always seemed to be at work. What on earth was he hiding?

We enjoyed the rest of the evening, and I spoke no more of Ravi's haggard-looking face. Even though I had enjoyed him biting because of his dishonesty, I had bigger fish to fry. That was two nights in a row that Ravi had lied to me, stayed out all night and claimed to be at his house. He pretended to have been home alone, when I knew full well that he had stayed out all night. I had cold hard evidence because I was there. My plan had been successful. I had found out that Ravi was hiding something. Mia seemed oblivious. Eric and Andy had seemed puzzled. What on earth was Ravi up to? His closest friends were not in the loop. Was Ravi wheeling and dealing? Was he involved in a business that I was unaware of? Some thinking time was needed. Ravi was never going to admit the truth. He was being secretive and elusive. He was a master of deception, and I did not want to cause an unnecessary storm if Ravi was negotiating private business. That was his affair. All I wanted to know was whether or not he was cheating on me. Nothing more. He knew fidelity was my non-negotiable. I could no longer trust Ravi. I couldn't just leave him though. I was only imagining that he had another woman, but I couldn't be 100% sure. What if I'd misread the whole situation? I decided that I needed to call in reinforcements.

9 THE P.I. AND THE PLAN

I don't recall what gave me the idea. Perhaps I'd watched one too many detective series box sets during the lockdowns. I researched a private investigator on the internet. I had no idea what I was doing. I picked the first one that popped up on screen. I felt anxious ringing the telephone number. It felt like I was doing something wrong. I would just enquire, see what was possible, if anything. The P.I. asked for my name, number and email address and I almost hung through sheer panic. I composed myself and gave him the details. I told the P.I. all about my suspicions, the two sleepovers, the secrecy and lies. "In my experience, from what you have told me, it sounds like he is definitely cheating on you. That is exactly the kind of behaviour I would expect from a man who is having an affair." I was both disappointed and relieved at the same time. There was probably nothing I could do without it verging on illegality. I explored options. Could I get access to his phone and read his messages? The P.I. said definitely not, that *would* be illegal. Could I perhaps track his car? The P.I. said that he believed that was the best solution. That way I could monitor Ravi's comings and goings myself and actually find out where he was spending Thursday nights. The P.I. told me that people usually stuck to certain routines and had habits, so I could observe Ravi's movements and spot patterns. The deal was made. The tracker was arranged. We agreed on a plan. That it would be fitted at 4am on Saturday. I had to be there to ensure that Ravi was in. I would definitely be at Ravi's on Friday night, so sometime throughout the night seemed the obvious choice.

Friday evening arrived. While I was out with Ravi and the gang, I felt a nervous tension. Did anyone know what I was up to? How could they? Did anyone suspect that Ravi was seeing someone else? Did I have trust issues? Was I going mad? I couldn't separate the truth from the lies. Different thoughts and mixed feelings were swimming around in my head. There were so many contradictions. The evening was as pleasant as usual and when Ravi and I got home, we went to bed, and Rav fell asleep almost immediately. I had a restless sleep, wondering if someone from the agency was on the drive, under Ravi's car, fitting the device. When I woke up the following morning I had no idea whether anyone had been to fit a tracker, or whether I had been scammed. As far as I knew, I could have paid the money to absolutely anyone. The money (quite a substantial sum) had gone out of my account. I had the emails. I had the paperwork. I crossed my fingers. I checked my phone at lunchtime and there it was. Details of how to log in and see where Ravi's car was at any given time. He was at work. I couldn't wait to finish work and get home to see where the tracker located him this evening. Friday – Work during the day, out for Fun Friday (obviously with me), then home until Saturday when he went to the clinic. It all checked out and corresponded to where we were and where I expected him to be. On Sunday we were at Ravi's as registered by the tracker, then I went home in the afternoon. I had followed the path of the tracker and was impressed how it logged our whereabouts and the journeys that Ravi's car made. It was time for me to go home so I could get ready for work the following day. Sunday late afternoon from Holmfirth, I had a quick check… I knew Rav would still be at home relaxing. I was wrong. Ravi was on the move! The tracker said that he was in …Loughborough…. Wait, What? I was in shock. Was the tracker accurate? I had left Ravi at home. He was relaxing at home that evening, yet his car was in Loughborough. How very odd. Had someone stolen his car? Had he had a sudden emergency. He had never mentioned friends or family in Loughborough. My mind was racing, and I felt a little panicked and confused. On Sunday evening he was still there. Perhaps it's a family member or friend that he hasn't mentioned. I have not listed every single one of my friends to him. He hasn't even met my friends. Don't jump to conclusions, G. Sit tight, play it cool. Keep calm. Sunday night: still in Loughborough. Late Sunday night: still in Loughborough. I had to go to bed. I had an early start the next day. There would be a reasonable explanation. I was quite restless that night and kept waking up to check the tracker. Loughborough. Loughborough. Loughborough. Loughborough. What the hell can he be doing in Loughborough? I eventually fell asleep and managed to grab a few hours before I had to get up for work. One quick glance at the tracker……. Loughborough! He stayed overnight. My heart sank. I knew that even if Ravi had a good reason, somehow my trust had been broken and if not completely broken it was certainly dwindling fast. If it was an emergency, then perhaps I did have serious trust issues. If not…, did I really want to find out the truth? I went to work, somewhat preoccupied with the whole situation, but as the day proceeded and I got increasingly engrossed in my tasks and chores, I came to the conclusion that I had to know. I had everything going for me. I was a strong independent woman. I was fine before I met Ravi. If the worst came to the worst and we broke up, I would be OK. Nothing to lose, I told myself. On Monday at 9am the tracker indicated that Ravi was at work. Afternoon: Gym. Evening: Home. OK. So back to the weekly routine. Had Ravi received an unexpected call from someone and gone out to Loughborough spontaneously? Yes, that was probably it. It would all be revealed as a last-minute visit or outing and my mind would be put to rest. I was in a hurry to get home that evening. Ravi usually called me on Monday evenings, but *I* called *him*. I couldn't wait for him to call me.

"Oh, hi, sweetheart. Is everything OK? You don't usually call me. How are you?"

"I'm fine. I just thought I'd ring you as I have a friend coming over tonight and didn't want you calling during her visit."

"Yeh, that's fine, sweetheart. No worries."

My friend was not visiting. Oh my god, I've turned into a liar. Overnight I have become a deceitful, deceptive, secretive, plotting, suspicious, dreadful girlfriend. I'll be asking to check his phone next. I am actually making up stories in my head. My imagination is running wild. My trust issues are bad. What the hell is wrong with me? What on earth am I doing? Ravi is so lovely. Am I trying to completely sabotage this amazing relationship? From my point of view, my voice was shaky and unnatural, and I tried to steady it before asking, "How was your Sunday?" My chest tightened.

"Sunday? Yesterday! You were with me on Sunday. What do you mean?"

What did I mean? I meant were you with another woman last night? "I meant…" Shall I come straight out with it? Shall I let the cat out of the bag? I mean I think you're cheating and every time I ask you about it, you deflect and lie. No. Stay true to yourself. He is clever. Keep calm. If he's honest, you'll be reassured with a completely acceptable answer and call off this whole ridiculous charade. Was it a mid -life crisis? Was it the dreaded menopause?…There was a lot about Perimenopause in the news lately, whatever that was…whatever the hell it was, I had to keep my head. "Well, when I left, did you watch anything interesting on TV?" Did that sound like a genuine, valid question? Banter? Chitchat? Could he sense that I was checking up on him?

"Oh, nothing much, I just watched a bit of the match," brilliant, all sounds natural, "and then I had an early night." Shocked, stunned silence on my part. "I was really tired after Saturday night. You tired me out," he laughed. And there it was. For a while I was certain that my instincts had been right. I did not have trust issues. Ravi was lying. How long had he been lying? What else had he lied about? Our relationship was so perfect. Could the tracker have been wrong? He sounded so genuine on the phone. Not caught out at all. I would ring the P.I. the following day. Yes, I needed a second opinion. I would touch base and explain my observations thus far and see what he had to say. The P.I. re-confirmed that cheats would establish a pattern, and I would see repetitive behaviour.

I thought about the P. I's words. "They usually stick to habit and have a routine. You will be able to see a pattern…probably on a weekly basis." Tuesday: Work. Gym. Home. Quick check before bedtime. Home. Wednesday: Work. Gym. Home. Thursday the same. A quick check before bedtime. Loughborough!!!! The next morning…Loughborough! Game on. I'm nobody's fool. This has been going on for too long. I was fed up of wasting my precious time on someone who was obviously not who they claimed to be. I was certain that Ravi was up to no good. I needed to get everything wrapped up over half-term. I wanted to close the matter once and for all, one way or another. I could get closure during the school holidays and then start afresh and bury myself in work to keep occupied. If it all blew up in my face, well, I would face the consequences. I had to get to the bottom of things. I just had to. I decided that I needed to inform the P.I. of my mission once I'd got the idea clear in my mind, just in case things went awry.

I set off. My plan was to go via Ravi's to pick up my things. By now, as well as a whole set of drawers and my own wardrobe at his place, I had shoes on the wrack by the porch, toiletries in the bathroom, and a few random belongings including books and ornaments around Ravi's house. As a last-minute thought, I grabbed a framed photograph from the mantlepiece. A photo of Ravi and I on holiday in Devon. Grinning like Cheshire cats, cheek to cheek, stood at the foot of a waterfall. I placed it carefully on the passenger seat. This was my visual proof. I checked the tracker. Ravi's car had stopped, and I now had a street address. I set off to Loughborough, with my car laden with belongings and the strange address that I had typed into my Sat Nav. I felt like a spy…a detective. I felt in control. Knowledge is power and I knew that Ravi was lying. About what, I was unsure, but it was enough for me to distrust him and cause a rift in our relationship. The journey seemed to take forever, and it was beginning to get dark. It was February. Over two years ago we had met. More than two years since first contact. What was I about to discover? An illicit den of inequity or a gang of money laundering criminals? (I had an overactive imagination, admittedly!) I started to feel scared and wondered if I was doing the right thing. I pulled into a service station and called the P.I. "Hi, it's Georgina."

"Hi, Georgina, any progress?"

"Actually, yes. Tonight is the night. I have tracked Ravi's car to the same location as before and I am going to confront him. I am going to remain calm and just make sure that he and this other woman are aware that I know exactly what is going on. I have been round to Ravi's and collected my stuff, so that will be the end of it. After tonight, you can remove the tracker."

"OK. Good luck. I hope you find your answers. I think you'll enjoy seeing the look on his face when you turn up on the doorstep. Take care, Georgina. Thank you for your business."

"Thank you. Thank you for listening and believing me. I will recommend you if ever any of my friends find themselves in a similar situation." As I approached Endgame Terrace and turned in, I could see Ravi's white BMW from a distance, parked half on, half off the pavement, as he always parked whenever we went anywhere. It always made me think of "half a cup" in the movie East is East. "Oh, my God. It's real. This is it! His car is there. This is it." The point at which my plan went awry was the fact that the tracker did not specify a house number and Ravi's car was parked in front of a trio of terraced houses in the cul de sac, slap bang in the middle. There were no other houses nor cars in sight. The row of houses stood in isolation, so I drove past so as not to be too conspicuous. I pulled up at the end of the road. It looked as though if I continued, it would lead me into the countryside. I was in the middle of nowhere. I turned the car around so I could see the houses, and more precisely Ravi's car. Which house was he in? I hedged my bets on the middle house. My heart beating faster, I got out of the car and walked up to the middle house. knocked on the door. No answer. I knocked again, more loudly. No answer. Maybe he's out? At the pub? Having dinner? Maybe it's not the right house. It was starting to get cold and dark. I went next door, to the house on the right. I knocked. A middle-aged man answered and asked, "Can I help you?"

"Oh, hello, sorry to bother you, I stammered. I was wondering if you know anything about the white BMW there.," I said as I turned round and pointed to Ravi's car.

"Why do you want to know?" He said defensively.

"It's just that it's my boyfriend's car and I'm wondering where he is."

"Oh. Oh. Right." He looked at me in a more pitiful manner. "Well, all I know is that he comes every week to visit her next door. He parks his car in the middle of the terrace, never says hello or smiles. We don't know her at all. She keeps herself to herself. I'm sorry I can't help you any more than that."

He saw my unamused face and continued, "I think they've gone out in her car. I'd stick around if I were you and try later." He 100% knew what the situation was here. I could tell. He smiled and I somehow felt like he was on my side. A car pulled up on the drive of the house to the left. My heart stopped. I didn't want to be caught off-guard. It was the neighbours to the other side of the middle house. They said hello in a friendly manner and went inside. Still no sign of Ravi. Thank goodness. I didn't want to be seen in the open by Ravi. I didn't want him to have any thinking time. I headed back to the car to collect my thoughts. So, it's not a criminal gang. Is it a secret second family, or a wife? I had to know. I got back to my car and waited. I got out of the car again and got my long puffa coat from the boot and put it on. It was bitterly cold now. Another hour or so passed, although it seemed like an eternity, and then a small boxy car approached from the opposite direction. The car pulled onto the middle drive. Bingo. I watched as two figures got out of the little vehicle. I recognised Ravi immediately. The other figure was female. Short and rather plump, so I knew it was not Mia. Mia was tall and slender. Who was she? Was it Nikki? My heart was pounding. They made their way to the front door, staggering and laughing. They went inside and the door closed. I was about to go and see what on earth was going on when it started to rain. Well, I'm not getting wet through, I thought. So, I turned on the engine and drove towards the middle house. I pulled up in front of Ravi's car and parked. I'll wait for the rain to stop and go and knock on the door. The rain lasted for ages and got heavier and heavier. I watched the lights upstairs go on and a few minutes later, off. So, they're all snuggled up in bed together and I'm out here in the cold.

When it finally stopped raining, I went to the door and knocked. No answer. I knocked loudly. Still no answer. I set my phone alarm for 6am and went to sleep in the car. I would surprise them both the next morning.

10 ENDGAME TERRACE

I spent a restless, uncomfortable night in my car, parked up all night on a small, unfamiliar street, in the middle of God only knows where, surrounded by my belongings. I felt like a drifter. As I awoke, I took a couple of minutes to compose myself and clear my head. I got out of the car and walked down the drive to resolve the matter once and for all. I knocked on the middle door. Silence. I knocked again, much louder this time, and could hear stirring. I waited patiently, photograph in hand. Let's go! The small chunky figure I had seen last night opened the door. She was wearing only a dressing gown. She looked sleepy and perplexed. "Hello?" She queried, rubbing her eyes.

I began with, "Hello, I'm ever so sorry to disturb you, but could you tell me whose car that is?" and I turned round and pointed to the prominent white vehicle that in the light of day stuck out like a sore thumb against the beautiful country landscape.

"That's my boyfriend's car," she answered defensively. "Why do you want to know?"

This was my moment. Keep calm, G! I was trembling slightly with both cold and nerves. "I would like to know because that is my boyfriend's car and I'm just wondering where on earth he is. I am guessing he's upstairs in your bedroom?"

She was stunned. "I'm sorry, what? *Who* are you?"

I thought I had made it quite clear, but apparently not. I raised the photograph from my thigh so she could see it and said, pointing at Ravi, grinning in the photo, "This is my boyfriend. This is us on holiday in Devon last Summer and I want to know what he is doing here. Would you like to ask him to come down so I can ask him myself?"

After a pause to get over the shock, she obviously had no idea that Ravi had a girlfriend, she screeched, "Ravi!!!" No answer. "Ravi get down here now," she screamed. No response. She turned to check if anyone was coming. Apparently not. "Come in," she said, and as she made her way upstairs, I followed her. As the small female went to open the bedroom door, she was met with an opposing force. She looked at me and I nodded. I stepped in front of the door next to her and we both pushed it open, forcing the body behind it to leap out of the way and seek cover in the far corner of the room. There he was a suddenly small and pathetic creature. A shadow of a man, shrunken in the furthest recess of the room. Cowering before the firing squad. Wearing only a pair of boxer shorts.

"You absolute piece of shit," I shouted. "I knew you'd been lying to me, but this just takes the biscuit. Trust issues? Yes, I have trust issues. Why do you think that might be, Ravi or should I call you Paul?"

"He told *me* his name was Paul as well when I first met him!" Exclaimed the mystery lady.

The love, admiration and respect that I had once felt for Ravi disintegrated in the blink of an eye. I still had the picture in my hand. Looking at my partner, guilty and unveiled in the corner, Vesuvius erupted. I threw the picture of us at his feet and as it landed on the floor, the glass shattered. The lady beside me began to cry. "I'm really sorry. I didn't want to get angry. I'll clean up the mess, don't worry." I raised my voice, "In fact, NO. Ravi, *you'll* clean up the mess!" Ravi nodded repeatedly. A feeble, deplorable form. The woman was very upset. I looked at her and gently said, "He's been playing us both. I'm his girlfriend. I suspected that he was cheating on me and when I asked him about it, he would gaslight me."

"I always said I thought you were cheating on me," cried the woman, looking at Ravi. "You're always looking at other women when we go out." she turned to me and sobbed, "He's always saying I'm too fat and should lose weight." Her flood gates really opened up.

"Well, you look fine to me. Just thank God we don't have to waste another single minute on this worthless piece of shit."

I faced Ravi and told him, "I'm going now. I'll collect all my stuff from yours and leave the key under the mat. Cross your fingers I don't trash the place."

Ravi looked worried. The woman suddenly shouted out, as though she'd had an epiphany, "Oh my God, she has a key? So, *I'm* the other woman!" She began to wail again.

"Come on, let's go downstairs and have a cup of tea." I said to her. "I've had a rough night, and I've now got some packing to do and a long journey ahead."

She nodded. We went downstairs and she filled the kettle with water.

"So, what's your name?" I asked.

"I'm Sye," she seemed to be calming down. "How long have you been with Ravi?"

"Two and a half years more or less. You?"

"Well on and off for about two years, but he was never available during school holidays, which I always found strange because his children are both young adults."

"I always stay with him at his place during school holidays, or we've gone away together."

"Are you a teacher?"

"Yes, did you have any suspicions?"

"Nothing I could ever identify or clarify. Rav always told me I was paranoid and had self-esteem issues."

"Dear God, this man is a real piece of work." I responded. " I don't even know who he is anymore. He's not the man I thought I'd met in the beginning. He's a lying, cheating scumbag."

As we were sharing stories, Sye called out, "And where do you think you're going?" I turned round to see Ravi creeping past the kitchen towards the front door. "Get back, you've got some explaining to do."

Ravi turned round and went back into the house. I got up and said to Sye, "I'll leave you to it. I've had enough; I'm done. Take care, Sye". I gave her a hug before leaving. I felt sorry for her. She actually believed that *she* was his girlfriend.

But I wasn't quite done. I wanted to apologise and say goodbye to Rob and Mia for suspecting Mia and acting coldly towards her at times. I called to let them know that something had happened, and I needed to come over and speak to them. They were shocked at first as I told them that I had suspected that Ravi had been seeing someone else and he had been more than deceitful about the whole affair. As I talked about the P.I. and the tracker Mia actually said, "You did the right thing, Georgie. Ravi has acted atrociously."

"Well, as well as saying sorry to you, Mia, for thinking you were the other woman, I wanted to make sure that you heard my side of things. I didn't just want to disappear and allow Ravi to invent a story. According to him, all his exes are mad. I didn't want to give him the opportunity to convince you of the same about me. It's been nice knowing you, but I doubt our paths will cross again."

"If you ever want to come to Ria's, your meal's on us, Georgie." Mia said sympathetically.

"And as much fizz as you can drink." Added Rob.

"Thanks, guys. That's kind of you. You never know. Look after each other. Bye."

I didn't dilly dally at Rob and Mia's as I wanted to go via Eric and Andy's to post a letter along with Ravi's key through their letterbox. That way, Ravi would know I'd dropped by. Mia and Rob were astute. I hoped they would let Ravi explain my absence and somehow drop himself in it. They knew the truth now, so they could provide Ravi with enough rope to hang himself, if they chose to. Would they even mention that I went to say goodbye to them? I would never know. At least if there ever *was* any funny business between Mia and Ravi, she now knew she wasn't the only other woman.

My letter to Eric and Andy simply said that I had caught Ravi cheating red-handed and that was a deal breaker for me. I had hired a P.I. because Ravi refused to tell the truth. I had met the other woman, and she seemed nice. Fragile, but nice. I insisted that Eric and Andy stay together forever and be kind to any of Ravi's future girlfriends. They were not to believe for one second that any of us, exes, future girlfriends or I were mad. I understood that Ravi was their friend, but as a partner, he was a damaged, manipulative, narcissistic compulsive liar. That was not bitterness. It was based on observation and experience.

By no means am I asking for pity. Don't feel sorry for me. I cried a river. I was upset. I was even heartbroken, but not over losing Ravi. I was glad that I had discovered Ravi's true nature. I was more disappointed about the fact that the man I fell in love with did not exist. The naturally handsome, well-aged, charming, genuine, loyal partner did not exist. Parts of Ravi were true, but not enough parts to make a whole person. I had begun to think of him as broken and damaged. I had been fooled from the very beginning. I had just chosen to ignore it. I felt strong that I had finally discovered the truth and walked away from the constant lies. So much of what Ravi said all knitted together in my mind to form a complex jigsaw puzzle of false narratives, tall stories and outright lies. This is not the kind of relationship I wanted to be tangled up in. Towards the end I found it hard to separate the truth from all Ravi's lies and I think I abandoned ship that first Thursday I spent the night at Ravi's alone. "Paul", 45 years old: Lies! G.P. and aesthetician: True. Staying out and cheating: Absolutely 100%. Another woman: Yes! Other women?: Probably…but I didn't care. I only needed to know about one. Who knows how many other women are caught up in his web of deceit.

The best part? Don't forget that I had two holidays booked under my name and pre-paid. Amalfi Coast plus a Mediterranean Cruise. Two holidays. Excellent holidays that were spent with good friends. The only thing I had to do was get the second name on the bookings changed. Helen and I enjoyed the cruise. It was great. Neither she nor I had ever been on a cruise before, so it was a whole brand-new adventure for us both.

I can thoroughly recommend visiting the Amalfi coast. It's absolutely beautiful. Tina came along with me on that particular holiday. She and I had an absolutely fantastic time.

The End?

Well,   almost…

ABOUT THE AUTHOR

The author has chosen to write this novella under a pen name. Why Georgie Bell? It has a good ring to it! Lol

Georgie's top tip: Plant Crocus, Muscari, Hyacinth, Daffodil and Tulip bulbs in Autumn. Plant them absolutely anywhere and everywhere. If you don't have a garden, plant them in pots. The joy you'll get when they pop up in Spring is priceless.

G.B.

Printed in Great Britain
by Amazon

61905890R00048